The Old Man and the Sea

Abridged From the Original Novel

老人與海 （原著刪節版）

Author Ernest Hemingway
Illustrator Julina Alekcangra

WORDS
1000

MP3

Let's Enjoy Masterpieces!

All the beautiful fairy tales and masterpieces that you have encountered during your childhood remain as warm memories in your adulthood. This time, let's indulge in the world of masterpieces through English. You can enjoy the depth and beauty of original works, which you can't enjoy through Chinese translations.

The stories are easy for you to understand because of your familiarity with them. When you enjoy reading, your ability to understand English will also rapidly improve.

This series of *Let's Enjoy Masterpieces* is a special reading comprehension booster program, devised to improve reading comprehension for beginners whose command of English is not satisfactory, or who are elementary, middle, and high school students. With this program, you can enjoy reading masterpieces in English with fun and efficiency.

This carefully planned program is composed of 5 levels, from the beginner level of 350 words to the intermediate and advanced levels of 1,000 words. With this program's level-by-level system, you are able to read famous texts in English and to savor the true pleasure of the world's language.

The program is well conceived, composed of reader-friendly explanations of English expressions and grammar, quizzes to help the student learn vocabulary and understand the meaning of the texts, and fabulous illustrations that adorn every page. In addition, with our "Guide to Listening," not only is reading comprehension enhanced but also listening comprehension skills are highlighted.

In the audio recording of the book, texts are vividly read by professional American actors. The texts are rewritten, according to the levels of the readers by an expert editorial staff of native speakers, on the basis of standard American English with the ministry of education recommended vocabulary. Therefore, it will be of great help even for all the students that want to learn English.

Please indulge yourself in the fun of reading and listening to English through *Let's Enjoy Masterpieces*.

海明威

Ernest Hemingway
(1899–1961)

Ernest Hemingway was an American novelist from Illinois. His earliest short stories, published in his high school newspaper, demonstrated his gift for storytelling. After graduation from high school, he decided to skip college and got a job working for a local newspaper as a journalist.

In 1918, Hemingway joined the Red Cross to participate in World War One. He was wounded on the Italian front and came back home. He then went to Europe as a foreign correspondent. While in Europe, Hemingway spent time with many famous writers, and he continued to write.

In 1923, his first book, *Three Short Stories and Ten Poems* was published. *A Farewell to Arms*, which came out in 1929, was essential to gaining him his literary reputation as a novelist. Published in 1952, *The Old Man and the Sea*, which describes an old fisherman's lonely struggle to catch a giant fish, received great critical acclaim. This novel was awarded the 1953 Pulitzer Prize and the Nobel Prize for Literature in 1954.

Ernest Hemingway died in July 1961. His death from a gunshot wound was considered to be a suicide. Hemingway is regarded as one of the 20th century's greatest writers.

The Old Man and the Sea exemplifies the spirit in life that Hemingway admired, described, and pursued. The story is about an old fisherman who finally catches a giant marlin after weeks of not catching anything. However, sailing homeward with the fish, he encounters sharks that devour the marlin's meat. By the time he returns to the harbor, only the skeleton of the fish is left.

This simple story's plot doesn't contain any big symbolism or great philosophy. Hemingway just vividly described a joyous triumph won in a relentless, agonizing battle, by using the story of an old man who would never cease his struggle.

As the old man says in the book, "A man can be destroyed but not defeated." The old man naturally tries hard to keep the giant marlin he has hooked and his epic endeavor exemplifies Hemingway's ideal that indomitable courage is the eternal triumph of the human spirit.

With simple and powerful language, Hemingway depicted the spirit of the fisherman and the dynamics of life. *The Old Man and the Sea* is praised as a crowning achievement for best exhibiting Hemingway's belief that although your life is a fight and defeat is the ultimate outcome, the dignity you will win during your struggle is a triumph worthy of respect.

HOW TO USE THIS BOOK

本書使用說明

① Original English texts

It is easy to understand the meaning of the text, because the text is rewritten according to the levels of the readers.

② Explanation of the vocabulary

The words and expressions that include vocabulary above the elementary level are clearly defined.

③ Response notes

Spaces are included in the book so you can take notes about what you don't understand or what you want to remember.

∩ Audio Recording

In the audio recording, native speakers narrate the texts in standard American English. By combining the written words and the audio recording, you can listen to English with great ease.

Audio books have been popular in Britain and America for many decades. They allow the listener to experience the proper word pronunciation and sentence intonation that add important meaning and drama to spoken English. Students will benefit from listening to the recording twenty or more times.

After you are familiar with the text and recording, listen once more with your eyes closed to check your listening comprehension. Finally, after you can listen with your eyes closed and understand every word and every sentence, you are then ready to mimic the native speaker.

Then you should make a recording by reading the text yourself. Then play both recordings to compare your oral skills with those of a native speaker.

HOW TO IMPROVE
READING ABILITY

如何增進英文閱讀能力

1 *Catch key words*

Read the key words in the sentences and practice catching the gist of the meaning of the sentence. You might question how working with a few important words could enhance your reading ability. However, it's quite effective. If you continue to use this method, you will find out that the key words and your knowledge of people and situations enables you to understand the sentence.

2 *Divide long sentences*

Read in chunks of meaning, dividing sentences into meaningful chunks of information. In the book, chunks are arranged in sentences according to meaning. If you consider the sentences backwards or grammatically, your reading speed will be slow and you will find it difficult to listen to English.

You are ready to move to a more sophisticated level of comprehension when you find that narrowly focusing on chunks is irritating. Instead of considering the chunks, you will make it a habit to read the sentence from the beginning to the end to figure out the meaning of the whole.

③ Make inferences and assumptions

Making inferences and assumptions is part of your ability. If you don't know, try to guess the meaning of the words. Although you don't know all the words in context, don't go straight to the dictionary. Developing an ability to make inferences in the context is important.

The first way to figure out the meaning of a word is from its context. If you cannot make head or tail out of the meaning of a word, look at what comes before or after it. Ask yourself what can happen in such a situation. Make your best guess as to the word's meaning. Then check the explanations of the word in the book or look up the word in a dictionary.

④ Read a lot and reread the same book many times

There is no shortcut to mastering English. Only if you do a lot of reading will you make your way to the summit. Read fun and easy books with an average of less than one new word per page. Try to immerse yourself in English as often as you can.

Spend time "swimming" in English. Language learning research has shown that immersing yourself in English will help you improve your English, even though you may not be aware of what you're learning.

CONTENTS

Introduction 4

How to Use This Book 6

How to Improve Reading Ability 8

Before You Read 12

Chapter One

The Worst Kind of Luck 14

Understanding the Story 32
Hemingway and *The Old Man and the Sea*

Chapter Two

Far Out to Sea 34

Comprehension Quiz 50

Chapter Three

The Battle Begins 52

Understanding the Story ················68

Man and Nature

Chapter Four

An Even Fight ···································· 70

Comprehension Quiz ·························· 94

Chapter Five

Shark Attack ····································· 96

Understanding the Story ··············110

The Caribbean Sea

Chapter Six

The Final Battle ····························· 112

Comprehension Quiz ························ 136

Appendixes

❶ Listening Guide ···························· 138

❷ Listening Comprehension ················ 142

Translation ····································· 144

Answers ··· 190

Before You Read

Old Man

I have been a fisherman all my life. I am old now, but I am still strong and determined. I am a master fisherman. That means I have a lot of knowledge about how to catch a fish. However, I have not caught a fish for many weeks. I know that I will catch a fish soon. So I go out in my boat every day and put out my fishing lines.

Boy

I live in Havana, near the beach with all the other fishermen. I learned how to fish when I was very young. The old man taught me everything I know about fishing. He is a great man, but my parents think he's unlucky. I believe he will catch a great fish again one day.

bow
船首

harpoon
魚叉

stern
船尾

fishing gear
釣魚用具

thole pin
（船邊）槳座

cast net
漁網

skiff
小型帆船

mast 帆柱
oar 船槳
gaff 搭鉤

fin 鰭

dorsal
背部的

pectoral
胸部的

sardine 沙丁魚
marlin 旗魚（馬林魚）
yellow jack 巴氏若鰺
bonito 鰹魚
shark 鯊魚

Chapter One

The Worst Kind of Luck

He was an old man who fished alone in a skiff[1] in the Gulf Stream[2] and he had gone eighty-four days without catching a fish.

During the first forty days without a fish the boy's parents had told him that the old man was now definitely[3] *salao* — the worst form of unlucky. The boy's parents had ordered him to go in another boat, which caught three good fish the first week.

---

1. **skiff** [skɪf] (n.) 輕舟；小艇
2. **the Gulf Stream**
   墨西哥灣流

3. **definitely** [ˋdefɪnətli] (adv.)
   無疑地；確定地
4. **gaff** [gæf] (n.) 搭鈎

It made the boy sad to see the old man come back each day with his skiff empty. He always went down to help him carry the lines, or the gaff[4] and harpoon[5] and the sail patched[6] with flour sacks[7], so that when it was furled[8], it looked like the flag of permanent[9] defeat[10].

The old man was thin and gaunt[11] with deep wrinkles[12] on the back of his neck and deep scars on his hands from handling lines of heavy fish. The dark spots of the benign[13] skin cancer that the tropical[14] sun brings were on his cheeks. His scars were as old as forgotten memories.

Everything about him was old except his eyes. They were the same color as the sea and were cheerful and undefeated.

5. **harpoon** [hɑːr`puːn] (n.) 魚叉
6. **patch** [pætʃ] (v.) 補釘
7. **flour sack** 麵粉袋
8. **furl** [fɜːrl] (v.) 捲起
9. **permanent** [`pɜːrmənənt] (a.) 永恆的；永遠的
10. **defeat** [dɪ`fiːt] (n.) 挫敗
11. **gaunt** [gɔːnt] (a.) 消瘦的
12. **wrinkle** [`rɪŋkl] (n.) 皺紋
13. **benign** [bɪ`naɪn] (a.) 良性的
14. **tropical** [`trɑːpɪkl] (a.) 熱帶的

"Santiago," the boy said to him, "I could go with you again. We've made some money[1]."

The old man had taught the boy to fish and the boy loved him.

"No," the old man said. "You're with a lucky boat. Stay there."

"But remember how you went eighty-seven days without fish and then we caught big ones every day for three weeks."

"I remember," the old man said. "I know you did not leave me because you doubted[2]."

1. **make money** 賺錢
2. **doubt** [daʊt] (v.)
   懷疑；不相信
3. **obey** [ə`beɪ] (v.) 服從；聽話
4. **faith** [feɪθ] (n.) 信念；信任
5. **offer** [`ɑːfər] (v.) 給予
6. **Terrace** [`terəs] (n.) 露台
7. **stuff** [stʌf] (n.) 東西

"It was papa who made me leave. I am a boy and I must obey[3] him."

"I know," the old man said. "He hasn't much faith[4]."

"No, but we have. Haven't we?"

"Yes. Can I offer[5] you a beer on the Terrace[6] and then we'll take the stuff[7] home."

"Why not?" the old man said. "Between fishermen."

They sat on the Terrace and many of the fishermen made fun of[1] the old man, but he was not angry. The older fishermen looked at him and were sad, but they did not show it.

The successful fishermen of that day had already butchered[2] their marlin[3] and carried them to the ice truck that would take them to the market in Havana[4].

Those who had caught sharks had taken them to the shark factory on the other side of the cove[5]. When the wind came from the East a smell came from the shark factory.

"Santiago," the boy said.

"Yes," the old man said. He was thinking of many years ago.

"Can I go out and get sardines[6] for you for tomorrow?"

"No. Go and play baseball. I can still row and Rogelio will throw the net[7]."

"I would like to go. If I cannot fish with you, I would like to serve[8] in some way."

"You bought me a beer," the old man said. "You are already a man." "How old was I when you first took me in a boat?"

"Five and you were nearly killed when I brought the fish in too green[9] and it nearly destroyed[10] the boat. Can you remember?"

1. **make fun of** 嘲弄；開玩笑
2. **butcher** [`butʃər] (v.) 屠宰
3. **marlin** [`mɑːrlɪn] (n.) 旗魚
   （又稱馬林魚，海中大型掠
   食性魚類的總稱）
4. **Havana** [hə`vænə] (n.)
   哈瓦那（古巴首都）
5. **cove** [kouv] (n.)
   小灣；小港
6. **sardine** [ˌsɑːr`diːn]
   (n.) 沙丁魚
7. **throw/cast a net** 撒網
8. **serve** [sɜːrv] (v.)
   服務；貢獻
9. **in (too) green** 時機未成熟
10. **destroy** [dɪ`strɔɪ] (v.) 毀滅

"I can remember the tail slapping[1] and the noise of the clubbing[2]."

"Can you really remember that?"

"I remember everything from when we went together."

The old man looked at him with his confident[3], loving eyes. "If you were my boy I'd take you out," he said. "But you are your father's and your mother's and you are in a lucky boat."

"May I get the sardines? I know where I can get four baits[4] too. "

"I have mine left from today."

"Let me get four fresh ones."

"One," the old man said. His hope and his confidence had never left him.

---

1. **slap** [slæp] (v.) 拍擊
2. **clubbing** [`klʌbɪŋ] (n.) 用棍棒打
3. **confident** [`kɑːnfɪdənt] (a.) 自信的
4. **bait** [beɪt] (n.) 餌

"Two," the boy said.

"Two," the old man agreed. "You didn't steal them?"

"I would," the boy said. "But I bought these."

"Thank you," the old man said. "Tomorrow is going to be a good day with this current[5]."

He was too simple to wonder when he had attained[6] humility[7].

But he knew it carried no loss of pride[8].

"Where are you going?" the boy asked.

"Far out. I want to be out before it is light."

5. **current** [ˋkɜːrənt] (n.) 潮流
6. **attain** [əˋteɪn] (v.) 獲得
7. **humility** [hjuːˋmɪləti] (n.) 謙遜

8. **pride** [praɪd] (n.) 自豪

"Are you strong enough now for a truly big fish?"

"I think so. And there are many tricks[1]."

"Let us take the stuff home," the boy said. "So I can get the cast net and go after[2] the sardines."

They picked up the things from the boat.

The old man carried the mast[3] on his shoulder[4] and the boy carried the wooden box with the fishing gear[5].

They walked to the old man's shack[6] and went in through its open door. The shack was made of the tough part of the royal palm[7] called *guano*[8].

In the shack there was a bed, a table, one chair and a place on the dirt[9] floor to cook with charcoal[10]. On the brown walls there was a color picture of the Sacred Heart of Jesus and another of the Virgin of Cobre[11], both relics[12] of his wife.

Once there had been a photograph of his wife on the wall but he had taken it down because it had made him lonely. Now it was on the shelf in the corner under his clean shirt.

1. **trick** [trɪk] (n.) 技巧
2. **go after** 跟在……後面
3. **mast** [mæst] (n.) 桅杆
4. **carry A on one's shoulder** 用肩扛著 A
5. **fishing gear** 釣具
6. **shack** [ʃæk] (n.) 簡陋的小屋
7. **royal palm** 〔植〕大王椰子
8. ***guano*** 西班牙文，指古巴蓋屋頂的棕櫚科植物
9. **dirt** [dɜːrt] (n.) 灰塵；穢物
10. **charcoal** [`tʃɑːrkoul] (n.) 木炭
11. **Virgin of Cobre** 又稱仁愛聖母（Virgin of Charity）古巴天主教的主保。
12. **relic** [`relɪk] (n.) 遺物

23

"What do you have to eat?" the boy asked.

"A pot of yellow rice with fish.

Do you want some?"

"No. I will eat at home. Do you want me to make a fire[1]?"

"No. I will make it later on."

"May I take the cast net?"

"Of course."

There was no cast net and the boy remembered when they had sold it. But they went through[2] this fiction[3] every day. There was no pot of yellow rice and fish and the boy knew this too.

"Eighty-five is a lucky number," the old man said. "How would you like to see me bring one in that weighed[4] over a thousand pounds?"

1. **make a fire** 生火
2. **go through** 經歷
3. **fiction** [ˋfɪkʃn] (n.) 虛構；謊言
4. **weigh** [weɪ] (v.) 重……（重量）

"I'll get the cast net and go for sardines. Will you sit in the sun in the doorway[5]?"

"Yes. I have yesterday's paper and I will read about baseball."

The boy did not know whether yesterday's paper[6] was fiction too. But the old man brought it out from under the bed.

"Perico gave it to me at the bodega[7]," he explained.

"I'll be back when I have the sardines. I'll keep yours and mine together on ice and we can share them in the morning. When I come back you can tell me about baseball. Now keep warm old man. Remember we are in September," the boy said.

"The month when the great fish come," the old man said. "Anyone can be a fisherman in May."

"I'm going for[8] the sardines now," the boy said.

---

5. **doorway** [ˈdɔːrweɪ] (n.) 門口
6. **paper** [ˈpeɪpər] (n.) 報紙
7. **bodega** [bəuˈdiːgə] (n.) 酒店
8. **go for** . . . 前往……

When the boy came back the old man was asleep[1] in the chair and the sun was down[2].

The boy took the old army blanket[3] off the bed and spread it over[4] the back of the chair and over the old man's strange but powerful shoulders.

His shirt had been patched[5] so many times that it was like a sail[6]. The old man's head was very old and with his eyes closed there was no life in his face. He was barefoot[7].

The boy left him there and when he came back the old man was still asleep.

"Wake up old man," the boy said.

The old man opened his eyes and for a moment he was coming back from a long way away.

Then he smiled.

"What have you got?" he asked.

"Supper," said the boy. "We're going to have supper."

"I'm not very hungry."

"Come on and eat. You can't fish and not eat."

"What are we eating?"

"Black beans and rice, fried bananas and some stew."

1. **asleep** [ə`sli:p] (a.) 睡著的
2. **the sun is down**
   太陽已經下山
3. **army blanket** 軍毯
4. **spread** A **over** B
   把 A 鋪在 B 上
5. **patch** [pætʃ] (v.)
   補釘；修補
6. **sail** [seɪl] (n.) 帆布
7. **barefoot** [`berfut]
   (a.) 赤足的

🎧 8

The boy had brought them in a metal container[1] from the Terrace.

"That's very kind of you," the old man said. "Should we eat?"

"I've been asking you to," the boy told him gently. "I didn't want to open the container until you were ready."

"I'm ready now," the old man said. "I only needed time to wash."

"Where did he wash?" the boy thought. The village water supply[2] was two streets down the road. I must have water here for him, and soap and a towel. Why am I so thoughtless[3]? I must get him another shirt and a jacket for the winter and some sort of shoes and another blanket.

"Your stew is excellent," the old man said.

"Tell me about baseball," the boy asked him.

"In the American League it is the Yankees as I said," the old man said happily.

"They lost[4] today," the boy told him.

"That means nothing. The great DiMaggio[5] is himself again."

"They have other men on the team."

"Naturally. But he makes the difference[6]," the old man said. "Do you remember when he used to[7] come to the Terrace? I wanted to take him fishing but I was too timid to ask him. Then I asked you to ask him and you were too timid.
I would like to take the great DiMaggio fishing. They say his father was a fisherman. Maybe he was as poor as we are and would understand."

"I used to sail on a big ship that went to Africa and I have seen lions on the beaches in the evening."

"I know. You told me."

1. **metal container** 金屬容器
2. **water supply** 供水
3. **thoughtless** [ˋθɔːtləs]
   (a.) 欠考慮的；粗心的
4. **lose** [luːz] (v.) 輸；失敗
   (lose-lost-lost)
5. **DiMaggio** Joseph Paul DiMaggio,1914/11/25 — 1999/3/8）美國職棒大聯盟傳奇球星，生涯都在紐約洋基隊渡過。
6. **make a difference** 使不同
7. **used to . . .** 過去時常……

"Should we talk about Africa or about baseball?"

"Baseball. Tell me about the great John Jota McGraw," the boy said.

"He used to come to the Terrace sometimes in the older days[1]. But he was rough and harsh-spoken[2] when he drank[3] too much."

"Who is the greatest manager[4], really, Luque or Mike Gonzalez?"

"I think they are equal[5]."

"And the best fisherman is you."

"No. I know others that are better."

"*Que va*[6]," the boy said, "There are many good fishermen and some great ones, but there is only you."

"Thank you. You make me happy. I hope no fish will come along so great that he will prove[7] us wrong."

"There is no such fish if you are still strong as you say."

"I may not be as strong as I think," the old man said. "But I know many tricks and I have resolution[8]."

The Old Man and the Sea

"You ought to go to bed now so that you will be fresh[9] in the morning."

"Good night then. I will wake you in the morning."

"You're my alarm clock," the boy said.

"Age is my alarm clock," the old man said. "Why do old men wake so early?

Is it to have longer days?"

"I don't know," the boy said. "All I know is that young boys sleep late and hard[10]. Sleep well, old man."

They had eaten with no light on the table.

The old man rolled his trousers up[11] to make a pillow, putting the newspaper inside them. He rolled himself in the blanket[12] and slept on the other old newspapers that covered[13] the springs[14] of the bed.

---

1. **in the older days**
   在過去的日子裡
2. **harsh-spoken** 言辭粗糙的
3. **drink** [drɪŋk] (v.) 喝酒
   (drink-drank-drunk)
4. **manager** [ˋmænɪdʒər] (n.)
   經理；經紀人
5. **equal** [ˋiːkwəl] (a.) 同等的
6. *que va* 〔西班牙語〕
   你說的是什麼話啊！
   (= What are you saying!)
7. **prove** [pruːv] (v.) 證明

8. **resolution** [ˌrezəˋluːʃn]
   (n.) 決心
9. **fresh** [freʃ] (a.) 有朝氣的
10. **sleep late and hard**
    睡得很晚很熟
11. **roll up** 捲起來
12. **roll oneself in the blanket**
    把自己捲在毯子裡
13. **cover** [ˋkʌvər] (v.) 覆蓋
14. **spring** [sprɪŋ] (n.) 彈簧

Hemingway and
The Old Man and the Sea

When Hemingway wrote *The Old Man and the Sea*, he was an old man himself. His previous novel was not a good book. But *The Old Man and the Sea* was instantly a huge success.

The simple, clear language Hemingway used to describe an old man's determination to succeed one more time appealed to many readers all over the world. Some people think that Hemingway was writing about himself, as a writer who wanted one more big success.

Many other people believe Hemingway based the character on Gregorio Fuentes, a Cuban who worked for the author. Fuentes was the captain of Hemingway's fishing boat, the Pilar, when Hemingway lived in Cuba.

However, Fuentes once told a reporter a different story. One day he and Hemingway were sailing on the Pilar when they saw an old fisherman. This man was in a small boat and had a large fish tied to the side. Hemingway told Fuentes he wanted to write about the fisherman.

Perhaps Hemingway combined parts of himself, his friends and people he saw to create the main character. After all, that could be why the story appeals to so many readers: the old man represents all men who struggle, determined to win just one more time.

· Chapter Two ·

Far Out to Sea

The old man dreamed of[1] Africa when he was a boy and the long, golden beaches. He lived along that coast[2] now every night and in his dreams he heard the surf[3] roar[4] and saw the native[5] boats come riding through[6] it.

As he slept he smelled the smell of Africa that the land breeze[7] brought in the morning.

1. **dream of** 夢見
2. **coast** [koʊst] (n.) 海岸
3. **surf** [sɜːrf] (n.) 浪花

4. **roar** [rɔːr] (v.) 怒號
5. **native** [ˋneɪtɪv] (a.) 當地的
6. **ride through** 乘著……航行

He no longer dreamed of storms, nor of women, nor of great events, nor of great fish, nor fights, nor contests of strength[8], nor of his wife.

Now he only dreamed of places and of the lions on the beach. They played like young cats in the dusk[9] and he loved them as he loved the boy. He never dreamed about the boy.

He woke up, looked out the open door at the moon and unrolled[10] his trousers and put them on. He went up the road to wake the boy.

The door of the house where the boy lived was unlocked[11] and the old man opened it and walked in quietly. He took hold of[12] the boy's foot gently and held it until the boy woke and turned and looked at him.

The old man nodded and the boy took his trousers from the chair by the bed and, sitting on the bed, pulled them on[13].

7. **breeze** [briːz] (n.) 微風
8. **contest of strength** 腕力比賽
9. **in the dusk** 在黃昏
10. **unroll** [ʌnˋroʊl] (v.) 攤開
11. **unlocked** [ʌnˋlɑːkt] (a.) 沒有鎖的
12. **take hold of** 握住
13. **pull on** 拉上

🎧 11

The old man went out the door and the boy came after[1] him. He was sleepy and the old man put his arm across his shoulders[2] and said, "I am sorry."

"*Que va*," the boy said. "It is what a man must do."

They walked down the road to the old man's shack and all along the road, in the dark, barefoot men were moving, carrying the masts[3] of their boats.

When they reached the old man's shack, the boy took the rolls[4] of line in the basket, the harpoon and gaff[5], and the old man carried the mast with the furled[6] sail on his shoulder.

"Do you want coffee?" the boy asked.

"We'll put the gear[7] in the boat and then get some."

They had coffee from condensed-milk[8] cans at an early morning place that served fishermen.

"How did you sleep old man?" the boy asked. He was waking up now although it was still hard for him to leave his sleep[9].

1. **come after** 跟在後面
2. **put one's arm across one's shoulders** 用手臂環住肩膀
3. **mast** [mæst] (n.) 船桅
4. **roll** [roʊl] (n.) 捲；綑
5. **gaff** [gæf] (n.) 搭鉤
6. **furled** [fɜːrl] (a.) 捲起的
7. **gear** [gɪr] (n.) 工具
8. **condensed-milk** 煉乳
9. **leave one's sleep** 離開夢鄉

"Very well, Manolin," the old man said. "I feel confident today."

"So do I," the boy said. "Now I must get your sardines and mine and your fresh baits."

"I'll be right back," the boy said. "Have another coffee. We have credit[1] here."

The old man drank his coffee slowly. It was all he would have all day and he knew that he should drink it. For a long time now eating had bored[2] him and he never carried a lunch.

He had a bottle of water in the bow[3] of the skiff and that was all he needed for the day.

The boy was back now with the sardines and the two baits, and they went down to the skiff, feeling the pebbled sand[4] under their feet[5]. They lifted the skiff and slid her into[6] the water.

1. **have credit** 允許賒帳
2. **bore** [bɔːr] (v.) 使無趣
3. **bow** [bau] (n.) 船首
4. **pebbled sand**
   粗糙帶著小石頭的沙灘
5. **feel *A* under one's feet**
   感覺 A 在腳下
6. **slide *A* into** 把 A 滑進······
7. **fit** [fɪt] (v.) 調整；配合
   (fit - fit/fitted - fit/fitted)

"Good luck, old man."

"Good luck," the old man said.

He fitted[7] the rope lashings[8] of the oars[9] onto the thole pins[10] and, leaning forward[11], he began to row out of the harbor in the dark.

There were other boats going out to sea and the old man heard the dip[12] and push of their oars even though he could not see them.

8. **lashing** [`læʃɪŋ] (n.) 捆綁
9. **oar** [ɔːr] (n.) 船槳
10. **thole pin** （船邊的）槳架
11. **lean forward** 往前傾靠
12. **dip** [dɪp] (n.) 下沈；傾斜

The old man knew he was going far out[1] and he left the smell of the land behind[2] and rowed out into the clean early morning smell of the ocean.

In the dark the old man could feel the morning coming and as he rowed he heard the sound of flying fish[3] leaving the water. He was very fond of[4] flying fish as they were his principal friends[5] on the ocean.

He was sorry for the birds, especially the small delicate[6] dark terns[7] that were always flying and looking and almost never finding.

And he thought, "The birds have a harder life than we do except for the robber[8] birds and the heavy strong ones. Why did they make birds so delicate and fine[9] as those sea swallows when the ocean can be so cruel? She is kind and very beautiful. But she can be so cruel[10]."

1. **go far out** 前往遠處
2. **leave A behind** 把 A 拋在後方
3. **flying fish** 飛魚
4. **be fond of** 喜歡
5. **principal friend** 重要的朋友
6. **delicate** [`delɪkət] (a.) 精巧的；纖細的
7. **tern** [tɜːrn] (n.) 燕鷗 (= sea swallow)
8. **robber** [`rɑːbər] (n.) 搶匪
9. **fine** [faɪn] (a.) 細緻的
10. **cruel** [kruːəl] (a.) 殘酷的

He always thought of the sea as *la mar* which is what people call her in Spanish when they love her. Sometimes those who love her say bad things about her but they always speak of the sea as though she were a woman.

Some of the younger fishermen, who had motor-boats, speak of her as *el mar* which is masculine[11]. They speak of her as a contestant[12] or a place or even as an enemy.

But the old man always thought of her as feminine[13] and as something that gave or withheld[14] great favors[15], and if she did wild or wicked[16] things it was because she could not help them. The moon affects her as it does a woman, he thought.

---

11. **masculine** [`mæskjəlɪn]
    (a.) 男性的;剛強的
12. **contestant** [kən`testənt]
    (n.) 競爭對手
13. **feminine** [`femənɪn]
    (n.) 女性

14. **withhold** [wɪθ`hoʊld]
    (v.) 保留;抑制
    (withhold-withheld-withheld)
15. **favor** [`feɪvər] (n.) 偏愛
16. **wicked** [`wɪkɪd] (a.) 邪惡的

He was rowing steadily[1] and it was no effort for him.

"Today I'll row out where the schools[2] of bonito[3] and albacore[4] are and maybe there will be a big one with them."

Before it was really light, he had his four baits out at different depths[5], and he was drifting[6] with the current. There was no part of the hook that a great fish could feel which was not sweet-smelling and good tasting.

The boy had given him two small fresh tunas which hung[7] on the two deepest lines and, on the others, he had a big blue runner[8] and a yellow jack[9].

Each line was as thick as a big pencil and was looped[10] onto a stick so that any pull or touch on the bait would make the stick dip[11].

Now the old man rowed gently to keep the lines straight[12] and at their proper depths.

1. **steadily** [ˋstedəli] (adv.) 平穩地；穩定地
2. **school** [skuːl] (n.) （魚）群
3. **bonito** [bəˋniːtau] (n.) 鰹魚
4. **albacore** [ˋælbəkɔː] (n.) 長鰭鮪（較小型的鮪魚）
5. **at different depths** 不同深度
6. **drift** [drɪft] (v.) 漂流
7. **hang** [hæŋ] (v.) 勾；掛 (hang-hung-hung)
8. **blue runner** 金鰺

The sun rose thinly from the sea and the old man could see the other boats, low on the water and well in toward the shore.

He looked down into the water and watched the lines that went straight down into the dark water. He kept them straighter than any other fisherman.

"I keep them with precision[13]," he thought. "Only I have no luck anymore." But who knows? Maybe today. Every day is a new day.

It is better to be lucky. But I would rather be exact. Then when luck comes you are ready.

Just then he saw a man-of-war bird[14] with his long black wings circling[15] in the sky ahead of him. He made a quick drop[16] and then circled again.

---

9. **yellow jack** [dʒæk] (n.) 巴氏若鰺
10. **loop** [luːp] (v.) 環繞;捲起
11. **dip** [dɪp] (v.) 下沈
12. **keep straight** 維持直的
13. **with precision** 維持精確度
14. **man-of-war bird** 軍艦鳥
15. **circle** [sɜːrkl] (v.) 繞圈
16. **drop** [drɑːp] (n.) 驟降

"He's got something," the old man said aloud. "He's not just looking."

"Dolphin[1]," the old man said aloud. "Big dolphin."

As the old man watched, a small tuna rose in the air[2], turned and dropped[3] into the water. Another and another rose and they were leaping[4] in long jumps after the bait.

After a while the stern[5] line became taut[6] under his foot.

He dropped his oars and felt the weight[7] of the small tuna's shivering[8] pull. He could see the blue back of the fish in the water as he pulled it in. The old man hit him on the head[9] for kindness and kicked him under the stern.

1. **dolphin** (a.) 這裡指 dolphin fish 鬼頭刀（鱰鰍）
2. **rise in the air** 升至空中
3. **drop** [drɑ:p] (v.) 落下
4. **leap** [li:p] (v.) 跳躍
5. **stern** [stɜ:rn] (n.) 船尾
6. **taut** [tɔ:t] (a.) 拉緊的
7. **weight** [weɪt] (n.) 重量
8. **shivering** [ˈʃɪvərɪŋ] (a.) 顫抖的
9. **hit** A **on the head** 擊打 A 的頭

"Albacore," he said aloud. "He'll make[1] a beautiful bait."

He did not remember when he first started talking to himself. Probably when the boy had left him, but he did not remember.

The sun was hot now and the old man felt it on the back of his neck, and felt the sweat trickle down[2] his back as he rowed. Just then, watching his lines, he saw one of the projecting[3] green sticks dip sharply[4].

"Yes," he said. "Yes," and he moved his oars inside the boat. He reached out for[5] the line and held it delicately[6] between the thumb and forefinger[7] of his right hand.

1. **make** [meɪk] (v.) 使；形成
2. **trickle down** 滴下
3. **projecting** [`prɑːdʒektɪŋ] (a.) 拋出的；凸出的
4. **sharply** [`ʃɑːrpli] (adv.) 猛烈地；激烈地
5. **reach out for** 伸手去拿

Then it came again. This time it was a tentative[8] pull and he knew exactly what it was. One hundred fathoms[9] below a marlin was eating the sardines that covered the point[10] of the hook.

This far out, he must be huge, he thought.

Eat them, fish. Please eat them. He felt the light delicate pull and then a harder pull when a sardine's head must have[11] been more difficult to break from the hook. Then there was nothing.

6. **delicately** [`dɛlɪkətli] (adv.)
   技巧精細地
7. **forefinger** [`fɔːrfɪŋgər]
   (n.) 食指
8. **tentative** [`tɛntətɪv] (a.)
   遲疑的；不確定的

9. **fathom** [`fæðəm] (n.)
   噚（測水深的單位，一噚為六呎，1.8288 公尺）
10. **point** [pɔɪnt] (n.) 尖端
11. **must have** + *p.p.*
    想必（對過去行為做推測）

"Come on," the old man said aloud. "Just smell them. Aren't they lovely? Eat them now and then there is the tuna. Don't be shy, fish. Eat them."

Then he felt something hard and unbelievably heavy. It was the weight of the fish and he let the line slip down[1], down, down. Now he was ready. He had three forty-fathom coils[2] of line in reserve[3], as well as the coil he was using.

"Eat it a little more," he said. "Eat it well."

Eat it so that the point of the hook goes into your heart and kills you, he thought. "Come up easy and let me put the harpoon into you. Are you ready? Have you been at the table[4] long enough?"

"Now!" he said aloud and struck[5] hard with both hands, gained a yard of line and then struck again and again, swinging with all the strength of his arms and the weight of his body.

1. **slip down** 往下滑
2. **coil** [kɔɪl] (n.) 一圈；一捲
3. **in reserve** 保留；預備
4. **at the table** 吃飯
5. **strike** [straɪk] (v.) 攻擊 (strike-struck-struck/stricken)

Nothing happened. The fish just moved away slowly and the old man could not raise him an inch. The boat began to move slowly toward the northwest. The fish moved steadily and they traveled slowly on the calm water.

"I wish I had the boy," the old man said aloud. "I'm being towed[6] by a fish. I must hold him all I can and give him the line when he wants it. Thank God he is traveling and not going down."

Four hours later the fish was still swimming out to sea, towing the skiff, and the old man was still braced[7] solidly[8] with the line across his back.

---

6. **tow** [toʊ] (v.) 拖；拉
7. **brace** [breɪs] (v.) 拉緊

8. **solidly** [ˋsɑːlɪdli] (adv.)
   有力地；堅固地

A True or False.

T F ❶ The old man was deeply pessimistic.

T F ❷ The old man lived on his fishing boat.

T F ❸ The old man was having a streak of bad luck.

T F ❹ The boy used to be the old man's apprentice.

T F ❺ The boy lived with the old man.

T F ❻ The old man usually dreams of his dead wife and lions.

B Rewrite the sentences with future continuous tense.

> The boy *helped* the old man get ready for the day's fishing.
> ⇨ The boy *will be helping* the old man get ready for the day's fishing.

❶ The old man hooked a huge fish.

⇨ _____

❷ The old man rowed far out to sea.

⇨ _____

❸ The tuna fish jumped out of the water.

⇨ _____

C Rearrange the following sentences in chronological order.

❶ The old man caught a tuna fish.

❷ The old man and the boy drank coffee together.

❸ A big fish ate the old man's bait.

❹ The old man's boat is towed far out to sea.

❺ The old man rowed far from land.

_____ ⇨ _____ ⇨ _____ ⇨ _____ ⇨ _____

D Fill in the blanks with the given words.

| made | trousers | dream | taut | current |

❶ The old man rolled up his _____.

❷ When the fish ate the hook, the line became _____.

❸ Tomorrow is going to be a good day to fish with this _____.

❹ The boy's father _____ him fish in another boat.

❺ At night, the old man would _____ of Africa.

[18]

The Battle[1] Begins

He looked behind[2] him and saw that no land was visible[3]. That makes no difference[4], he thought. I can always come in on the glow[5] from Havana. Maybe he will come up before sunset, or with the moon.

I have no cramps[6] and I feel strong. It is he that has the hook in his mouth. But what a fish to pull like that. I wish I could see him only once to know what I have against[7] me.

The fish never changed his course[8]. It was cold after the sun went down. He tied the sack[9] that covered the bait box around his neck so that it hung down[10] over his back and he cautiously[11] worked it down under the line that was across his shoulders now.

I can do nothing with him and he can do nothing with me, he thought.

Once he stood up and urinated[12] over the side of the skiff and looked at the stars and checked his course. They were moving more slowly now and the glow of Havana was not so strong, so he knew the current must be carrying them eastward.[13]

1. **battle** [`bætl] (n.) 戰役
2. **look behind** 往後看
3. **visible** [`vɪzəbl] (a.) 可見的
4. **make no difference**
   沒什麼影響
5. **glow** [gloʊ] (n.) 熾熱；光輝
6. **cramp** [kræmp] (n.) 抽筋
7. **against** [ə`ɡeɪnst] (prep.)
   面對；與……競爭
8. **course** [kɔːrs] (n.)
   路線；方向
9. **sack** [sæk] (n.) 袋子
10. **hang down** 懸；掛
11. **cautiously** [`kɔːʃəsli] (adv.)
    留心地；注意地
12. **urinate** [`jʊrəneɪt] (v.) 小便
13. **eastward** [`iːstwərdz]
    (adv.) 向東方地

I wonder how the baseball came out[1] in the grand leagues[2] today, he thought. It would be wonderful to do this with a radio. Think of what you are doing. You must do nothing stupid.

Then he said aloud, "I wish I had the boy to help me and to see this."

No one should be alone in their old age[3], he thought. But it is unavoidable[4]. I must remember to eat the tuna before he spoils[5] in order to keep strong. Remember, you must eat him in the morning, he said to himself.

1. **come out** 結果;演變
2. **league** [liːg] (n.) 聯盟
3. **in one's old age** 在老年
4. **unavoidable** [ˌʌnəˈvɔɪdəbl] (a.) 不可避免的
5. **spoil** [spɔɪl] (v.) 腐壞 (spoil-spoilt/spoiled-spoilt/spoiled)
6. **porpoise** [ˈpɔːrpəs] (n.) 鼠海豚
7. **come around** 來到附近
8. **blow** [bloʊ] (v.) 噴水 (blow-blew-blown)
9. **make a joke** 開玩笑
10. **one another** 彼此

During the night two porpoises[6] came around[7] the boat and he could hear them rolling and blowing[8].

"They are good," he said. "They play and make jokes[9] and love one another[10]. They are our brothers like the flying fish."

Then he began to pity[1] the great fish that he had hooked[2]. He is wonderful and strange and who knows how old he is, he thought. Never have I had such a strong fish nor one who acted so strangely. Perhaps he is too wise to jump. He could ruin[3] me by jumping.

But what a great fish he is and what he will bring in the market if the flesh[4] is good. He took the bait like a male and he pulls like a male[5] and his fight has no panic[6] in it. I wonder if he has any plans or if he is just as desperate[7] as I am."

1. **pity** [ˋpɪti] (v.) 同情；憐憫
2. **hook** [hʊk] (v.) 鉤住
3. **ruin** [ˋruːɪn] (v.) 毀滅
4. **flesh** [flɛʃ] (n.) 肉
5. **male** [meɪl] (n.) 男性
6. **panic** [ˋpænɪk] (n.) 驚慌
7. **desperate** [ˋdɛspərət] (a.) 絕望的
8. **settle** [ˋsɛtl] (v.) 坐下
9. **join** [dʒɔɪn] (v.) 連結；作伴
10. **surge** [sɜːrdʒ] (n.) 大浪；波濤

"I wish the boy were here," he said aloud and settled[8] himself against the bow and felt the strength of the great fish through the line he held across his shoulders.

"My choice was to go out to find him beyond all people in the world. Now we are joined[9] together and no one to help either one of us."

The fish made a surge[10] that pulled him down[11] on his face and made a cut[12] below his eye.

The blood ran down his cheek a little way. But it coagulated[13] and dried before it reached his chin[14] and he worked his way[15] back to the bow and rested against[16] the wood.

11. **pull _A_ down** 把 A 往下拉
12. **cut** [kʌt] (n.) 割傷
13. **coagulate** [kouˈægjuleɪt] (v.) 凝結
14. **chin** [tʃɪn] (n.) 下巴
15. **work one's way** 努力前進
16. **rest against** 靠在……休息

I wonder why he made that surge, he thought. The wire must have slipped[1] on the great hill of his back. Certainly his back cannot feel as bad as mine does. But he cannot pull this skiff forever, no matter how[2] great he is.

"Fish," he said softly, aloud, "I'll stay with you until I am dead."

When the sun had risen further the old man realized that the fish was not getting tired[3]. There was only one favorable[4] sign. The slant[5] of the line showed he was swimming at a lesser depth[6]. That did not mean that he would jump. But he might.

"God, let him jump," the old man said. "I have enough line to handle[7] him."

"Fish," he said, "I love you and respect you very much. But I will kill you dead before this day ends."

A small bird came toward the skiff from the North. He was a warbler[8] and the old man could see he was very tired. He flew around the old man's head and rested on the line.

"How old are you?" the old man asked the bird. "Is this your first trip?" The bird was very tired and he teetered[9] on the line as his delicate feet gripped[10] it.

"Take a good rest, small bird," he said. "Then go and take your chance[11] like any man or bird or fish."

1. **slip** [slɪp] (v.) 滑動;滑落
2. **no matter how** 無論如何
3. **get tired** 變得疲倦
4. **favorable** [`feɪvərəbl] (a.) 有利的
5. **slant** [slænt] (n.) 傾斜
6. **at a lesser depth** 在比較淺的深度
7. **handle** [`hændl] (v.) 應付;處理
8. **warbler** [`wɔːrblər] (n.) 鶯
9. **teeter** [`tiːtər] (v.) 站不穩
10. **grip** [grɪp] (v.) 夾住;緊握
11. **take one's chance** 抓住機會

Just then the fish gave a sudden lurch[1] that pulled the old man down to the bow and would have pulled him overboard[2] if he had not braced himself and given some line.

The bird flew away and he felt the line carefully with his right hand and noticed his hand was bleeding[3]. Shifting[4] the weight of the line to his left shoulder and kneeling carefully, he washed his hand in the ocean.

The cut was in the working part of his hand. He knew he would need his hands before this was over and he did not like to be cut before it started.

"Now," he said, "I must eat the small tuna."

He knelt down[5] and found the tuna under the stern. He put one knee on the fish and cut strips[6] of dark red meat from the back of the head to the tail.

1. **lurch** [lɜːrtʃ] (n.)
   突然搖晃；傾斜
2. **overboard** [`ouvərbɔːrd]
   (adv.) 船外；落水
3. **bleed** [bliːd] (v.) 流血
   (bleed-bled-bled)
4. **shift** [ʃɪft] (v.) 移轉
5. **kneel down** 跪下
6. **strip** [strɪp] (n.)
   一片；一條
7. **cramped** [kræmpt] (a.)
   抽筋的

"I don't think I can eat an entire one," he said. He could feel the steady hard pull of the line and his left hand was cramped[7].

"What kind of a hand is that," he said. Cramp then if you want. Make yourself into a claw. It will do you no good[8]."

He picked up a piece of tuna and put it in his mouth and chewed it slowly. It was not unpleasant[9].

"How do you feel, hand?" he asked the cramped hand that was almost as stiff[10] as rigor mortis[11]. "I'll eat some more for you."

I wish I could feed the fish, he thought. He is my brother. But I must kill him and keep strong to do it. Slowly he ate all the strips of fish.

"God help me to have the cramp go," he said. "Because I do not know what the fish is going to do.

What is his plan, he thought. And what is mine?

---

8. **do A no good** 對 A 沒好處
9. **unpleasant** [ʌn`plɛznt] (a.) 令人不愉快的
10. **stiff** [stɪf] (a.) 僵硬的
11. **rigor mortis** [rɪgər mɔːrtəs] (ph.) 【醫】屍僵；死後強直

23

His left hand was still cramped, but he was unknotting[1] it slowly.

I hate cramps, he thought. It is a treachery[2] of one's own body. Then, with his right hand he felt the difference in the pull of the line.

"He's coming up," he said. "Come on hand. Please come on."

The line rose slowly and steadily and then the surface of the ocean bulged[3] ahead of the boat and the fish came out. He came out unendingly[4] and water poured[5] from his sides. He was bright in the sun and his head and his sides were wide and colored a light lavender[6].

His sword[7] was as long as a baseball bat and tapered[8] like a rapier[9], and he rose his full length[10] from the water and then re-entered it, smoothly, like a diver and the old man saw the great scythe-blade[11] of his tail go under[12], and the line started to race out[13].

1. **unknot** [ʌnˋnɑːt] (v.) 解開
2. **treachery** [ˋtretʃəri] (n.) 背叛；不忠
3. **bulge** [bʌldʒ] (v.) 膨脹；突起
4. **unendingly** [ʌnˋendŋli] (adv.) 無盡地；無終止地
5. **pour** [pɔːr] (v.) 傾注；傾瀉
6. **light lavender** 淡紫羅蘭色
7. **sword** [sɔːrd] (n.) 武器；劍
8. **taper** [ˋteɪpər] (v.) （物體的一端）逐漸變尖細

"He is two feet longer than the skiff," the old man said. He was trying with both hands to keep the line just inside of breaking strength. He knew that if he could not slow the fish with a steady pressure, the fish could take out [14] all the line and break it.

9. **rapier** [ˋreɪpɪər]
   (n.) 細長輕巧的劍
10. **full length** 全長
11. **scythe-blade** [saɪð bleɪd]
    長柄大鐮刀般的魚鰭
12. **go under** 往下
13. **race out** 全速被拉走
14. **take out** 帶走

63

He is a great fish but I must convince[1] him that he is no match[2] for me, he thought. I must never let him learn his strength nor what he could do if he made his run[3].

The old man had seen many great fish. He had seen many that weighed more than a thousand pounds and he had caught two of that size in his life, but never alone.

Now alone, and out of sight of[4] land, he was tied fast[5] to the biggest fish that he had ever seen and bigger than he had ever heard of, and his left hand was still cramped.

1. **convince** [kənˋvɪns]
   (v.) 說服
2. **match** [mætʃ] (n.)
   對手；敵手
3. **make one's run** 開始跑
4. **out of sight of**
   在視線外
5. **fast** [fæst] (adv.)
   緊緊地；牢固地

6. **suffering** [ˋsʌfərɪŋ]
   (a.) 受苦的
7. **not . . . at all** 完全不……
8. **religious** [rɪˋlɪdʒəs]
   (a.) 有宗教信仰的
9. **pilgrimage** [ˋpɪlgrɪmɪdʒ]
   (n.) 朝聖

I wonder why he jumped, the old man thought. He jumped almost as though to show me how big he was. I wish I could show him what sort of man I am. But then he would see the cramped hand.

At noon the old man's left hand was uncramped. He was comfortable but suffering[6], although he did not admit the suffering at all[7].

"I am not religious[8]," he said. "But I will say ten Our Fathers and ten Hail Marys so that I can catch this fish, and I promise to make a pilgrimage[9] to the Virgin de Cobre if I catch him. Christ, I did not know he was so big."

"I'll kill him though," he said. "In all his greatness."

Although it is unjust[1], he thought. But I will show him what a man can do and what a man endures[2].

"I told the boy I was a strange old man," he said. "Now is when I must prove[3] it."

The thousand times that he had proved it meant nothing. Now he was proving it again.

"If you're not tired, fish," he said aloud, "you must be very strange."

He felt very tired now and he tried to think of other things. He thought of the Big Leagues[4], and he knew the Yankees of New York were playing the Tigers of Detroit.

This is the second day that I do not know the result of the *juegos*[5], he thought. But I must have confidence[6] and I must be worthy of[7] the great DiMaggio who does all things perfectly.

Do you believe the great DiMaggio would stay with a fish as long as I will stay with this one? he thought. I am sure[8] he would and more since he is young and strong. Also his father was a fisherman.

1. **unjust** [ˌʌnˋdʒʌst]
   (a.) 不公平的
2. **endure** [ɪnˋdʊr]
   (v.) 忍受；忍耐
3. **prove** [pruːv] (v.) 證明
4. **Big League** 大聯盟

5. *juegos* 遊戲（西班牙文）
6. **have confidence** 有信心
7. **be worthy of**
   值得；配得上
8. **I am sure (that) . . .**
   我肯定……

Man and Nature

As far back as ancient cave paintings, art has been strongly influenced by Nature. Ever since humans became aware of Nature, they have sometimes thought of Her as a competitor or as a provider.

Throughout human history, natural forces have caused great hardship and loss of life. On both land and sea, humankind has had to battle nature to survive. This struggle is represented in different types of art throughout the centuries.

For example, Beethoven's "Sixth Symphony" expresses the violence of a thunderstorm. Herman Melville's novel *Moby Dick* is a masterpiece in literature that depicts the struggle between a man and Nature. Hemingway's *The Old Man and the Sea* is another example of this theme.

However, Hemingway's old man is not always fighting Nature. Nature provides the old man with food. Even a lost bird provides the old man with some company in his lonely battle.

The old man does not regard Nature as his enemy. Instead he thinks of the sea as a woman who changes her mood frequently. Sometimes she is kind and loving, but sometimes she is cruel and unforgiving.

Chapter Four

🎧26 An Even[1] Fight

As the sun set, to give himself more confidence, he remembered the time in the tavern[2] at Casablanca when he had played the hand game[3] with the great negro[4] from Cienfuegos, who was the strongest man on the docks[5].

They had gone one day and one night with their elbows on a chalk line on the table. Each one was trying to force the other's hand down onto the table. They changed the referee[6] every four hours so that the referees could sleep.

1. **even** [`ɪːvn] (a.) 對等的
2. **tavern** [`tævərn] (n.) 小酒館
3. **play the hand game**
   比腕力
4. **negro** [`niːgrou] (n.)
   （貶）黑人
5. **dock** [dɑːk] (n.) 碼頭
6. **referee** [ˌrefəˋriː] (n.) 裁判
7. **odds** [ɑːdz] (n.) 機率
8. **back and forth** 來來回回
9. ***El Campeon***
   冠軍（西班牙文）

The odds[7] would change back and forth[8] all night. Once the negro had the old man, who was not an old man then but was Santiago *El Campeon*[9], nearly three inches off balance[10].

But the old man had raised his hand again. He was sure then that he had the negro, who was a fine man and a great athlete[11], beaten[12].

And at daylight[13] he had forced the hand of the negro down and down until it rested on the table. The match had started on a Sunday morning and ended on a Monday morning.

10. **off balance** 失去平衡
11. **athlete** [ˋæθliːt] (n.) 運動員
12. **beaten** [biːtn] (a.) 被打敗的
13. **at daylight** 白晝

71

🎧 27

For a long time everyone had called him "The Champion." After that he had a few matches[1] and then no more. He decided that he could beat[2] anyone if he wanted to badly[3] enough and he decided that it was bad for his right hand for fishing.

1. **match** [mætʃ] (n.) 比賽
2. **beat** [biːt] (v.) 打敗
   (beat-beat-beaten)
3. **badly** [ˋbædli] (adv.) 非常地
4. **weed** [wiːd] (n.) 這裡指海草
5. **jump in the air** 在空中跳躍
6. **flap** [flæp] (v.) 拍打；拍動
7. **lean over** 傾身；曲身

Just before it was dark, as they passed a great island of Sargasso weed[4], his small line was taken by a dolphin. He saw it first when it jumped in the air[5], bending and flapping[6] wildly.

When it was at the stern the old man leaned over[7] and lifted the burnished[8] gold fish with its purple spots[9] over the stern.

Its jaws[10] were working convulsively[11] in quick bites against the hook. It pounded[12] the bottom of the skiff with its long flat body, its tail and its head until he clubbed it. Then it shivered[13] and was still[14].

The old man watched the sun go into the ocean and the slant of the big cord.

"He hasn't changed at all," he said.

But watching the movement of the water against his hand he noted[15] that it was a bit slower.

---

8. **burnished** [ˋbɜːrnɪʃt]
   (a.) 光滑的
9. **spot** [spɑːt] (n.) 斑點
10. **jaw** [dʒɔː] (n.) 上下顎
11. **convulsively** [kənˋvʌlsɪvli]
   (adv.) 痙攣性地
12. **pound** [paʊnd] (v.) 猛擊
13. **shiver** [ˋʃɪvər] (v.) 顫抖
14. **still** [stɪl] (a.) 靜止不動的
15. **note** [noʊt] (v.) 注意；留意

"I'll lash[1] the two oars together across the stern and that will slow him in the night," he said. "He's good[2] for the night and so am I."

I'm learning how to do it, he thought. This part of it anyway. Then, too, remember he hasn't eaten since he took the bait[3] and he is huge and needs much food. I have eaten the whole bonito[4]. Tomorrow I will eat the dolphin.

The Old Man and the Sea

"How do you feel[5], fish?" he asked aloud. "I feel good and my left hand is better and I have food for a night and a day. Pull the boat, fish."

He did not truly feel good because the pain from the cord across his back had almost passed pain and gone into a dullness[6] that worried him.

But I have had worse things than that, he thought. My hand is only cut a little and the cramp is gone[7] from the other. My legs are all right.

It was dark now as it becomes dark quickly after the sun sets in September. The first stars were out[8]. He did not know the name of Rigel[9] but he saw it and knew that soon they would all be out and he would have all his distant[10] friends.

1. **lash** [læʃ] (v.) 用繩索綁起來
2. **be good** 有利的;有益的
3. **take the bait** 吞下誘餌
4. **bonito** [bə`ni:tau] 鰹魚 (n.)
5. **How do you feel?**
   你覺得如何?
6. **dullness** [dʌlnəs]
   (n.) 麻木;無感覺
7. **be gone** 消失
8. **be out** 消逝;不見
9. **Rigel** [`raɪgəl](n.)〔天〕參宿七
   (獵戶星座其中一顆星)
10. **distant** [`dɪstənt] (a.) 遠方的

75

"The fish is my friend too," he said aloud. "I have never seen or heard of such a fish.

But I must kill him. I am glad we do not have to try to kill the stars."

Then he was sorry for the great fish that had nothing to eat and his determination[1] to kill him never relaxed[2] in his sorrow[3] for him.

How many people will he feed, he thought. But are they worthy to eat him? No, of course not. There is no one worthy of[4] eating a fish with such great dignity[5].

The old man rested for what he believed to be two hours. The moon did not rise until late now and he had no way of[6] judging the time. He was still bearing[7] the pull of the fish across his shoulders.

"But you have not slept yet, old man. It is half a day and a night and now another day and you have not slept," he said aloud. "I must devise[8] a way so that you sleep a little if he is quiet and steady. If you do not sleep you might become unclear in the head."

I could go without sleeping, he told himself. But it would be too dangerous.

He worked his way back to the stern. The stars were bright now and he saw the dolphin clearly and he pushed the blade of his knife into his head and pulled him out from under the stern.

The dolphin was cold and gray-white now in the starlight[9] and the old man skinned[10] one side of him while he held his right foot on the fish's head. Then he skinned the other side and cut fillets[11]. He leaned over the side and put his hand in the water. The flow[12] of the water against it was less strong.

"He is tired or he is resting. Now let me eat this dolphin and get some rest and a little sleep."

1. **determination** [dɪ,tɜːrmɪneɪʃn] (n.) 決心
2. **relax** [rɪˋlæks] (v.) 鬆懈
3. **sorrow** [ˋsɔːrou] (n.) 遺憾
4. **worthy of** 應得；值得
5. **dignity** [ˋdɪgnəti] (n.) 尊嚴；自尊
6. **have no way of . . .** 沒有辦法……
7. **bear** [ber] (v.) 忍受 (bear-bore-borne)
8. **devise** [dɪˋvaɪz] (v.) 想出；策畫
9. **in the starlight** 在星光下
10. **skin** [skɪn] (v.) 剝皮
11. **fillet** [ˋfɪlɪt, fɪˋleɪ] (n.) 魚片
12. **flow** [flou] (n.) 流動

（30）

Under the stars he ate half of one of the dolphin fillets.

"What an excellent fish dolphin is to eat cooked[1]," he said. "And what a miserable[2] fish raw[3]. I will never go in a boat again without salt or limes[4]."

1. **cooked** [kʊkt] (a.) 煮熟的
2. **miserable** [ˋmɪzrəbl] (a.) 令人難受的
3. **raw** [rɔ:] (a.) 生的
4. **lime** [laɪm] (n.) 萊姆
5. **cloud** [klaʊd] (v.) 遮蔽；覆蓋
6. **one after another** 一個接一個
7. **canyon** [ˋkænjən] (n.) 峽谷

The sky was clouding[5] over to the East and one after another[6] the stars he knew were gone. It looked now as though he were moving into a great canyon[7] of clouds and the wind had dropped[8].

"There will be bad weather in three or four days," he said. "But not tonight or tomorrow. Rig[9] now to get some sleep, old man, while the fish is calm and steady. "

The moon had been up for a long time but he slept on and the fish pulled on steadily[10] and the boat moved into the tunnel of clouds.

He woke with the jerk[11] of his right fist coming up against his face and the line burning out[12] through his right hand. He could not feel the line with his left hand but he braked[13] all he could with his right and the line rushed out.

8. **drop** [drɑ:p] (v.) 停止
9. **rig** [rɪg] (v.)
   裝置（船上）設備
10. **steadily** [ˋstedəli]
    (adv.) 平穩地

11. **jerk** [dʒɝːrk] (n.) 猛然一動
12. **burn out** 發熱
13. **brake** [breɪk] (v.) 煞住

Finally his left hand found the line and he leaned back[1] against it and now it burned his back and his left hand. His left hand was taking all the strain[2] and it was cutting badly.

Just then the fish jumped making a great bursting of the ocean and then a heavy fall. Then he jumped again and again, and the boat was going fast although line was still racing out[3], and the old man was raising the strain to the breaking point[4]. He had been pulled down tight on to the bow and his face was in the cut slice of dolphin and he could not move.

This is what we waited for, he thought. So now let us take it. Make him pay for[5] the line. Make him pay for it."

1. **lean back** 往後靠
2. **strain** [streɪn] (n.) 張力
3. **race out** 跑走；急速減少
4. **to the breaking point**
   幾乎被扯斷
5. **pay for ...** 為⋯⋯付出代價
6. **splash** [splæʃ] (n.) 濺水聲
7. **get one's head up**
   把頭抬高
8. **be on one's knees** 跪下
9. **rise to one's feet** 站起身

He could not see the fish's jumps but only heard the breaking of the ocean and the heavy splash[6] as he fell. The speed of the line was cutting his hands badly but he had always known this would happen.

If the boy were here he would wet the coils of line, he thought. Yes. If the boy were here.

The line went out but it was slowing now and he was making the fish earn each inch of it. Now he got his head up[7] from the wood and out of the slice of fish that his cheek had crushed. He was on his knees[8] and then he rose to his feet[9]. He was giving line but more slowly all the time.

I wonder what started him so suddenly? Could it have been hunger that made him desperate, or was he frightened[1] by something in the night?

Maybe he suddenly felt fear. But he was such a calm, strong fish and he seemed so fearless and so confident. It is strange.

"You better be fearless and confident yourself, old man," he said.

The old man held him with his left hand and stooped down[2] and scooped up[3] water in his right hand to get the crushed dolphin flesh off his face[4]. He was afraid that it might nauseate[5] him and cause him to vomit[6] and lose his strength[7].

He washed his right hand in the water and then let it stay in the salt water while he watched the first light come before the sunrise.

1. **be frightened** 害怕；驚嚇
2. **stoop down** 曲身；彎腰
3. **scoop up** 舀起
4. **get** *A* **off one's face**
   把臉上的 A 撥掉
5. **nauseate** [ˋnɔːsieɪt]
   (v.) 感到噁心
6. **vomit** [ˋvɑːmɪt] (v.) 嘔吐
7. **lose one's strength**
   喪失力量

He's headed almost East, he thought. That means he is tired and going with the current. Soon he will have to circle. Then our true work begins.

After he judged that his right hand had been in the water long enough he took it out and looked at it.

"It is not bad," he said. "And pain does not matter[8] to a man."

He took hold of[9] the line carefully so that it did not fit into any of the fresh line cuts and shifted[10] his weight so that he could put his left hand into the sea on the other side of the skiff.

8. **matter** [ˋmætər]
 (v.) 要緊；重要
9. **take hold of** 握住

10. **shift** [ʃɪft] (v.) 移轉

"You did not do so badly for something worthless[1]," he said to his left hand. "But there was a moment when I could not find you."

Why was I not born with[2] two good hands? he thought. Perhaps it was my fault in not training the left one properly. But God knows he had enough chances to learn. He did not do so badly in the night, though, and he has cramped only once. If he cramps again let the line cut him off.

The sun was rising for the third time since he had set out[3] to sea when the fish started to circle[4].

"It is a very big circle," he said. "But he is circling."

I must hold all I can, he thought. The strain will shorten his circle each time. Perhaps in an hour I will see him. Now I must convince him and then I must kill him.

1. **worthless** [ˋwɝːθləs]
   (a.) 無價值的
2. **be born with** 與生俱來
3. **set out** 啟程
4. **circle** [ˋsɝːrkl] (v.) 繞圈
5. **be wet with sweat**
   因流汗而濕透
6. **be tired deep into one's bones** 極為疲累
7. **salt** [sɔːlt] (v.) 給……加鹽
8. **feel faint and dizzy**
   覺得暈眩

But the fish kept on circling slowly and the old man was wet with sweat[5] and tired deep into his bones[6] two hours later. But the circles were much shorter now and from the way the line slanted he could tell the fish had risen steadily while he swam.

For an hour the old man had been seeing black spots before his eyes and the sweat salted[7] his eyes and salted the cut under his eye and on his forehead. He was not afraid of the black spots. Twice, though, he had felt faint and dizzy[8] and that had worried him.

"I cannot fail and die on a fish like this," he said. "Now that[1] I have him coming so beautifully. God help me endure[2]. I'll say a hundred Our Fathers and a hundred Hail Marys. But I cannot say them now."

Consider[3] them said, he thought. I'll say them later.

Just then he felt a sudden banging[4] and jerking on the line he held with his two hands. It was sharp and heavy.

He is hitting the wire with his sword, he thought. He may jump and I would rather he circled now. The jumps were necessary for him to take air[5]. But after that each jump can widen[6] the opening[7] of the hook wound[8] and he can throw the hook.

"Don't jump, fish," he said. "Don't jump."

The fish hit the wire several times more, and each time the old man gave up a little line.

After a while the fish stopped beating at the wire and started circling slowly again. The old man was gaining line steadily now. But he felt faint again. He lifted some sea water with his left hand and put it on his head. Then he put more on and rubbed the back of his neck.

"I have no cramps," he said. "He'll be up soon and I can last[9]. You have to last. Don't even speak of it."

He kneeled against the bow and, for a moment, slipped the line over his back again.

I'll rest now while he circles and then stand up and work on him when he comes in, he decided.

1. **now that** 既然
2. **endure** [ɪnˋdʊr] (v.) 忍受
3. **consider** [kənˋsɪdər] (v.) 認為
4. **banging** [bæŋɪŋ] (n.) 重擊聲
5. **take air** 獲得空氣
6. **widen** [ˋwaɪdn] (v.) 使變寬
7. **opening** [oʊpnɪŋ] (n.) 縫隙；開口
8. **wound** [wuːnd] (n.) 傷口
9. **last** [læst] (v.) 堅持

I'm more tired than I have ever been, he thought, and now the trade wind[1] is rising. But that will be good to take him in with.

The sea had risen considerably[2]. But it was a fair weather[3] breeze and he had to have it to get home."

"I'll just steer[4] south and west," he said. "A man is never lost[5] at sea and it is a long island."

It was on the third turn that he saw the fish for the first time. He saw him first as a dark shadow that took so long to pass under the boat that he could not believe its length[6].

"No," he said. "He can't be[7] that big."

But he was that big and at the end of this circle he came to the surface[8] only thirty yards away and the man saw his tail out of the water. It was higher than a big scythe blade and a very pale lavender above the dark blue water.

1. **trade wind** 季節風
2. **considerably**
   [kən`sɪdərəblɪ] (adv.)
   頗為；相當高地
3. **fair weather** 舒適的天氣
4. **steer** [stɪr] (v.) 掌舵；行進
5. **be lost** 迷失；迷路
6. **length** [lɛŋθ] (n.) 長度
7. **can't be . . .**
   不可能會是⋯⋯
8. **come to the surface**
   來到表面
9. **bulk** [bʌlk] (n.) 體積；大小
10. **stripe** [straɪp] (n.) 條紋

As the fish swam just below the surface the old man could see his huge bulk[9] and purple stripes[10]. His dorsal[11] fin[12] was down and his huge pectorals[13] were spread wide[14]. Then the old man could see the fish's eye.

The old man was sweating now but from something else besides the sun. On each placid[15] turn the fish made, he was gaining line and he was sure that in two turns he would have a chance to get the harpoon in.

11. **dorsal** [`dɔːrsl] (a.) 背部的
12. **fin** [fɪn] (n.) 鰭
13. **pectoral** [`pɛktərəl]
　　(n.) 胸肌；胸鰭
14. **be spread wide** 伸展得極寬
15. **placid** [`plæsɪd]
　　(a.) 平靜的；溫和的

89

But I must get him close[1], close, close," he thought. I mustn't try for[2] the head. I must get the heart.

"Be calm and strong, old man," he said.

The fish was coming in on his circle now calm and beautiful with only his great tail moving. The old man pulled on him to bring him closer. For just a moment the fish turned a little on his side. Then he straightened[3] himself and began another circle.

"I moved him," the old man said. "I moved him then."

He felt faint again but he held on to the great fish with all his strength[4].

I moved him, he thought. Maybe this time I can get him over[5].

Pull, hands, he thought. Hold up[6], legs. Last for me, head. Last for me. You never went. This time I'll pull him over.

1. **get** *A* **close** 讓 A 靠近
2. **try for** 想辦法達到……
3. **straighten** [ˋstreɪtn] (v.) 變直
4. **with all one's strength** 用盡力氣
5. **get** *A* **over** 終結 A
6. **hold up** 保持強壯
7. **put forth** 提出；使出
8. **right** [raɪt] (v.) 修正；使恢復正常

But when he put forth[7] all of his effort, the fish righted[8] himself and swam away.

"Fish," the old man said. "Fish, you are going to have to die anyway. Do you have to kill me too?"

That way nothing is accomplished[1], he thought. His mouth was too dry to speak but he could not reach for[2] the water now.

I must get him alongside[3] this time, he thought. I am not good for many more turns.

Yes, you are, he told himself. You're good forever.

On the next turn, he nearly had him. But again the fish righted himself and swam away slowly.

You are killing me, fish, the old man thought. But you have a right to. Never have I seen a greater, or more beautiful or a calmer or more noble[4] thing than you, brother. Come on and kill me. I do not care[5] who kills who.

Now you are getting confused[6] in the head, he thought. You must keep your head clear and know how to suffer like a man or a fish.

1. **accomplish** [əˋkɑːmplɪʃ] (v.) 完成；達到
2. **reach for** 拿到
3. **alongside** [əˏlɔːŋˋsaɪd] (adv.) 在旁邊；並排地
4. **noble** [ˋnoʊbl] (a.) 高貴的
5. **care** [ker] (v.) 在乎
6. **get confused** 變得混亂
7. **clear up** 澄清
8. **mushy** [ˋmʌʃi] (a.) 柔軟的
9. **flash** [flæʃ] (n.) 閃光

"Clear up, head," he said in a voice he could hardly hear. "Clear up[7]."

He tried it once more and he felt himself going when he turned the fish. The fish righted himself and swam off again slowly with the great tail moving in the air.

I'll try it again, the old man promised, although his hands were mushy[8] now and he could only see well in flashes[9].

A True or False.

T F ❶ The old man does not respect the fish he caught.

T F ❷ His left hand has cramped only once.

T F ❸ The old man's hero is Joe DiMaggio.

T F ❹ The old man wanted the big fish to jump to make his hook wound wide.

T F ❺ By the time the old man had the fish close to the boat, he was near the end of his strength.

B Choose the correct answer.

❶ Choose the sentence that best describes the old man.

(a) He's one to give up easily.

(b) He will fight to his last breath.

(c) He likes to have expensive and fancy things.

(d) He complains too much.

❷ What happened to the old man's left hand?

(a) It became cramped.

(b) It was bleeding very much.

(c) He crushed it under the oar.

(d) It was cut off from the pressure of the fishing line.

C Fill in the blanks with the given words.

poured   lurch   as long as   strange   fillets

❶ He cut the dolphin up into _____.

❷ Water _____ from the sides of the fish when it jumped.

❸ The fish's sword was _____ a baseball bat.

❹ The old man said to the boy, "I am a _____ old man."

❺ The big fish surprised the old man with a powerful _____.

D Rearrange the sentences in chronological order.

❶ The big fish jumped.

❷ The old man got some sleep.

❸ The old man ate some of the dolphin.

❹ A small bird visited the old man.

❺ The old man remembered that he had won an arm-wrestling contest.

_____ ⇨ _____ ⇨ _____ ⇨ _____ ⇨ _____

Chapter Five

🎧 38 Shark Attack

He took all his pain and what was left of his strength and his long-gone[1] pride and he put it against the fish's agony[2].

The fish came over onto his side and swam gently[3] and started to pass the boat.

The old man dropped the line and put his foot on it and lifted the harpoon as high as he could and drove it down with all his strength into the fish's side just behind the great chest fin[4].

He felt the iron go in and he leaned[5] on it and drove it further and then pushed all his weight after[6] it.

Then the fish came alive, with his death in him, and rose high out of the water showing all his great length and width[7] and all his power and his beauty. He seemed to hang in the air above the old man in the skiff. Then he fell into the water with a crash[8].

1. **long-gone** 消失已久的
2. **agony** [ˋægəni]
   (n.) 極大的痛苦
3. **gently** [ˋdʒentli]
   (adv.) 溫和地
4. **chest fin** 胸鰭
5. **lean** [liːn] (v.) 傾斜；倚靠
6. **push all one's weight after**
   用盡全力推向……
7. **width** [wɪdθ] (n.) 寬度
8. **crash** [kræʃ]
   (n.) 巨大的衝擊聲

The old man felt faint[1] and sick and he could not see well. But he cleared[2] the harpoon line and let it run slowly through his raw[3] hands and, when he could see, he saw the fish was on his back with his silver belly[4] up.

The shaft[5] of the harpoon was projecting[6] at an angle[7] from the fish's shoulder and the sea was red with the blood from his heart. The fish was silvery[8] and still and floated[9] with the waves. The old man laid his head on his hands.

"Keep my head clear," he said. "I am a tired old man. But I have killed this fish which is my brother and now I must do the slave work[10]."

1. **faint** [feɪnt] (a.) 快要暈倒的
2. **clear** [klɪr] (v.) 清理；使乾淨
3. **raw** [rɔ:] (a.) 擦傷的；刺痛的
4. **belly** [ˋbeli] (n.) 腹部
5. **shaft** [ʃæft] (n.) 箭尖
6. **project** [prəˋdʒekt] (v.) 投擲
7. **at an angle** 從一種角度

Now I must prepare the rope to tie him alongside the skiff, he thought. This skiff will never hold[11] him.

He started to pull the fish in[12] to have him alongside the skiff. I want to see him, he thought, and to touch and to feel him.

He is my fortune[13], he thought. But that is not why I wish to feel him. I think I felt his heart when I pushed on the harpoon the second time. Bring him in now and get the noose[14] around his tail and another around his middle to tie him to the skiff.

8. **silvery** [ˋsɪlvəri] (a.) 銀色的
9. **float** [floʊt] (v.) 漂浮
10. **slave work** 苦工
11. **hold** [hoʊld] (v.) 支撐住
(hold-held-held)
12. **pull** *A* **in** 把 A 拖進⋯⋯
13. **fortune** [ˋfɔːrtʃuːn] (n.) 財產
14. **noose** [nuːs] (n.) 繩索

"Get to work, old man," he said. He took a very small drink of[1] water.

"There is much slave work to do now that the fight is over[2]."

He looked up at[3] the sky and then out to his fish.

"Come on, fish," he said. But the fish did not come. Instead he lay[4] there and the old man pulled the skiff up to him.

When the fish's head was against the bow[5] he could not believe his size.

"It was the only way to kill him," the old man said. He was feeling better and his head was clear. He's over fifteen hundred pounds, he thought. Maybe much more.

"I think the great DiMaggio would be proud of me today."

1. **take a drink of . . .**
   喝一口……
2. **over** [`oʊvər] (a.) 結束的
3. **look up at** 往上看……
4. **lie** [laɪ] (v.) 躺；橫臥
   (lie-lay-lain)
5. **bow** [baʊ] (n.) 船頭
6. **fasten to** 綁在……
7. **stern** [stɜːrn] (n.) 船尾
8. **thwart** [θwɔːrt]
   (n.) 船上的座板
9. **lash** [læʃ] (v.) 用繩索綁

The Old Man and the Sea

He fastened[6] the fish to the bow, to the stern[7] and to the middle thwart[8]. He was so big it was like lashing[9] a much bigger skiff alongside.

He could see the fish and he had only to look at his hands and feel his back against the stern to know that this had truly happened and was not a dream.

41

They were sailing together lashed side by side[1] and the old man thought, let him bring me in if it pleases[2] him. I am only better than him through trickery[3] and he meant[4] me no harm.

It was an hour before the first shark hit him. The shark had come up[5] from deep down in the water as the dark cloud of blood had settled[6] and dispersed[7] in the mile-deep sea.

He had come up so fast that he broke[8] the surface of the blue water and was in the sun. Then he fell back into the sea and picked up[9] the scent[10] and started following the skiff and the fish.

1. **side by side** 並排；一起
2. **please** [pli:z] (v.)
   使愉悦；使高興
3. **trickery** [ˋtrɪkəri]
   (n.) 詭計；取巧
4. **mean** [mi:n]
   (mean-meant-meant)
   (v.) 存心；意圖
5. **come up** 游上來
6. **settle** [ˋsetl] (v.) 下降
7. **disperse** [dɪˋspɜːrs]
   (v.) 散開
8. **break** [breɪk] (v.) 打破
   (break-broke-broken)
9. **pick up** 找到
10. **scent** [sent] (n.) 氣味

🎧 42

Sometimes he lost the scent. But he would pick it up again and he swam fast and hard. He was a very big Mako shark built[1] to swim as fast as the fastest fish in the sea and everything about him was beautiful except his jaws[2].

His back was as blue as a swordfish's[3] and his belly was silver and his hide[4] was smooth[5] and handsome. Inside the closed double lip of his jaws all of his eight rows[6] of teeth were slanted[7] inwards[8]. They were not the ordinary pyramid-shaped[9] teeth of most sharks.

They were shaped like a man's fingers when they are curled[10] like claws. They were nearly as long as the fingers of the old man and they had razor-sharp[11] cutting edges[12] on both sides.

When the old man saw him coming he knew that this was a shark that had no fear at all and would do exactly what he wished.

He prepared the harpoon and the rope while he watched the shark come forward.

The old man's head was clear and good now and he was full of resolution[13] but he had little hope.

It was too good to last, he thought. It might as well[14] have been a dream.

I cannot keep him from hitting me but maybe I can get him. *Dentuso*, he thought. Bad luck to your mother.

1. **built** [bɪlt] (a.)
   有……構造的
2. **jaw** [dʒɔ:] (n.) 顎
3. **swordfish** [ˋsɔːrdfɪʃ]
   (n.) 旗魚
4. **hide** [haɪd] (n.) 皮
5. **smooth** [smu:θ] (a.) 光滑的
6. **row** [rou] (n.) 排；列
7. **slant** [slænt] (v.) 傾斜
8. **inwards** [ɪnwərdz]
   (adv.) 向內地
9. **pyramid-shaped**
   金字塔形的
10. **curl** [kɜ:rl] (v.) 使捲曲
11. **razor-sharp**
    像剃刀一樣銳利的
12. **cutting edge** 切口
13. **resolution** [ˌrezəˋlu:ʃn]
    (n.) 決心
14. **might as well** 也同樣可能

When the shark hit the fish, the old man saw his mouth open and his strange eyes. He heard the clicking[1] sound of the teeth as he tore[2] into the meat just above the tail.

He rammed[3] the harpoon down into the shark's head and into his brain. He hit it with his bloody hands, driving the harpoon with all his strength. He hit it without hope but with resolution and complete malignancy[4].

The shark swung[5] over and the old man saw his eye was not alive. The old man knew that he was dead but the shark would not accept it. It ploughed[6] over the water as a speed-boat[7] does. Then he lay quietly for a little while and went down very slowly.

"He took about forty pounds and my harpoon," the old man said. He did not like to look at the fish any more since he had been mutilated[8]. When the fish had been hit, it was as though[9] he himself were hit.

1. **clicking** [ˋklɪkɪŋ] (n.) 喀嚓聲
2. **tear** [ter] (v.) 撕扯；撕裂 (tear-tore-torn)
3. **ram** [ræm] (v.) 猛撞；推擠
4. **malignancy** [məˋlɪgnənsi] (n.) 敵意；惡意
5. **swing** [swɪŋ] (v.) 擺動 (swing-swung-swung)
6. **plough** [plaʊ] (v.) 破浪前進

It was too good to last, he thought. I wish it had been a dream now and that I had never hooked[10] the fish and was alone in bed on the newspapers.

"But man is not made for defeat," he said. "A man can be destroyed but not defeated[11]."

I am sorry that I killed the fish though, he thought. Now the bad time is coming and I do not even have the harpoon.

"Don't think, old man," he said aloud. "Sail on and take it when it comes."

7. **speed-boat** 快艇
8. **mutilate** [`mju:tɪleɪt] (v.) 毀壞；殘缺不全
9. **as though** 如同；彷彿
10. **hook** [hʊk] (v.) 釣上
11. **defeat** [dɪ`fi:t] (v.) 擊敗

He knew quite well the pattern[1] of what could happen when he reached the inner part of the current[2]. But there was nothing to be done now.

"Yes, there is," he said aloud. "I can lash my knife to the butt[3] of one of the oars."

So he did that. "Now, I am still an old man. But I am not unarmed[4]." He watched only the forward part of the fish and some of his hope returned.

It is silly not to hope, he thought. Besides I believe it is a sin. Do not think about sin[5]. There are enough problems now without sin.

I have no understanding of[6] it and I am not sure that I believe in it. Perhaps it was a sin to kill the fish. I suppose it was though I did it to keep me alive and feed many people. But then everything is a sin. Do not think about sin. You were born to[7] be a fisherman.

You did not kill the fish only to keep alive and to sell for food, he thought.

You killed him for pride and because you are a fisherman. You loved him when he was alive and you loved him after. If you love him it is not a sin to kill him. Or is it more?

But you enjoyed killing the *dentuso*, he thought.

"I killed him in self-defense[8]," the old man said aloud. "And I killed him well."

Besides, he thought, everything kills everything else in some way. Fishing kills me exactly as it keeps me alive. The boy keeps me alive. I must not deceive[9] myself too much.

1. **pattern** [`pætərn]
   (n.) 模式；樣式
2. **current** [`kɜːrənt]
   (n.) 洋流；海流
3. **butt** [bʌt] (n.) 較粗的一端
4. **unarmed** [ˌʌn`ɑːrmd]
   (a.) 徒手的；無武器的
5. **sin** [sɪn] (n.) 罪惡；罪孽
6. **have no understanding of . . .** 對⋯⋯不了解
7. **be born to . . .** 天生⋯⋯
8. **self-defense** 自衛
9. **deceive** [dɪ`siːv] (v.) 欺騙

The Caribbean Sea

The three largest of the major seas are, in order of size, South China, Mediterranean and Caribbean. The South China Sea is commonly featured in today's headlines as China, Vietnam, Malaysia and the Philippines and each try to control the resources found there.

The Mediterranean was very important in the development of early Western civilization.

Finally, the Caribbean is famous for its clear waters, beautiful coral and abundant marine life. It is also famous as the setting for Hemingway's *The Old Man and the Sea*.

The Caribbean is a favorite destination for tourists who enjoy fishing, scuba diving, relaxing on white beaches or swimming in clear blue waters. Many islands that used to be colonies of European nations are located there.

Cuba is the largest of these islands, and is unique as one of the last surviving socialist nations. The capital of Cuba, Havana, is featured in Hemingway's story. This capital used to be a famous tourist destination for rich and famous Americans, but since socialist government took power, Havana lost its appeal as a tourist destination.

Chapter Six

The Final Battle

🎧45

He had been sailing for two hours when he saw the first of the two sharks.

"*Galanos*[1]," he said aloud.

He took up the oar with the knife lashed to it. He lifted it as lightly as he could because his hands rebelled at[2] the pain, and he watched the sharks come.

They were hateful sharks, bad-smelling scavengers[3] as well as killers, and when they were hungry they would bite at an oar or the rudder[4] of a boat.

"*Ay*," the old man said. "*Galanos*. Come on, *Galanos*."

They came. One turned and went out of sight[5] under the skiff and the old man could feel the skiff shake as he jerked[6] and pulled on the fish. The other watched the old man with his yellow eyes and then came in fast to hit the fish where he had already been bitten.

A line showed clearly on the top of his brown head and back where the brain joined the spinal cord[7] and the old man drove the knife on the oar into the brain, withdrew[8] it, and drove it in again into the shark's yellow cat-like eyes. The shark let go of the fish and slid[9] down, swallowing[10] what he had taken as he died.

---

1. *Galanos* 西班牙文，指 shovel-nosed sharks（鏟鼻鯊）
2. **rebel at . . .** 對……反感
3. **scavenger** [`skævɪndʒər] (n.) 以腐屍為食的動物
4. **rudder** [`rʌdər] (n.) 船舵
5. **go out of sight** 失去蹤影
6. **jerk** [dʒɜːrk] (v.) 猛推
7. **spinal cord** 脊髓
8. **withdraw** [wɪθ`drɔː] (v.) 抽回 (withdraw-withdrew-withdrawn)
9. **slide** [slaɪd] (v.) 滑動 (slide-slid-slid)
10. **swallow** [`swɑːlou] (v.) 吞下

When he saw the other shark he leaned over the side and punched him. The blow[1] hurt his hands and his shoulder. But the shark came up fast with his head out and the old man hit him squarely[2] in the center of his flat-topped[3] head.

The old man withdrew the blade[4] and punched the shark exactly in the same spot[5] again. The old man stabbed[6] him in his left eye, but the shark still hung[7] there.

1. **blow** [blou] (n.) 一擊
2. **squarely** [`skwerli] (adv.) 筆直地
3. **flat-topped** 頂部平坦的
4. **blade** [bleɪd] (n.) 刀；刃
5. **spot** [spɑːt] (n.) 部位；位置
6. **stab** [stæb] (v.) 刺
7. **hang** [hæŋ] (v.) 逗留；徘徊 (hang-hung-hung)

"No?" the old man said and he drove the blade between the vertebrae[8] and the brain and he felt the cartilage[9] break.

"Go on, *galano*. Slide down a mile deep. Go and see your friend, or maybe it's your mother."

The old man wiped[10] the blade of his knife and laid down[11] the oar. Then he brought the skiff on to her course.

8. **vertebra** [`vɑːrtɪbrə]
   (n.) 脊椎骨
   （複數 vertebrae）
9. **cartilage** [`kɑːrtɪlɪdʒ]
   (n.) 軟骨

10. **wipe** [waɪp] (v.) 擦淨
11. **lay down** 放下

"They must have taken a quarter of him and of the best meat," he said aloud. "I wish it were a dream and that I had never hooked him. I'm sorry about it, fish. It makes everything wrong." He stopped and he did not want to look at the fish now.

"I shouldn't have gone out so far, fish," he said. "Neither for you nor for me. I'm sorry, fish. God knows how much that last one took," he continued. "But she's much lighter now." He did not want to think of the mutilated[1] underside of the fish.

He was a fish to keep a man all winter, he thought. Don't think of that. Just rest and try to get your hands in shape[2] to defend what is left of him. The next shark that came was a single shovel-nose[3].

1. **mutilated** [ˋmjuːtəleɪt] (adj.) 殘缺不全的
2. **in shape** 在正常狀態
3. **shovel nose** 形狀像鏟子的鼻子
4. **trough** [trɔːf] (n.) 飼料槽
5. **snap** [snæp] (v.) 啪地一聲折斷
6. **sink** [sɪŋk] (v.) 下沈 (sink-sank/sunk-sunk/sunken)
7. **gaff** [gæf] (n.) 搭鉤
8. **tiller** [ˋtɪlər] (n.) 船柄
9. **club** [klʌb] (n.) 棍；棒

He came like a pig to the trough[4] if a pig had a mouth so wide that you could put your head in it. The old man let him hit the fish and then drove the knife on the oar down into his brain. But the shark jerked backwards as he rolled and the knife blade snapped[5].

The old man did not even watch the big shark sinking[6] slowly in the water.

"I have the gaff[7] now," he said. "But it will do no good. I have the two oars and the tiller[8] and the short club[9]."

Now they have beaten me, he thought. I am too old to club sharks to death. But I will try it as long as I have the oars and the short club and the tiller.

🎧 48

It was getting late in the afternoon and he saw nothing but the sea and the sky.

"You're tired, old man," he said. "You're tired inside." The sharks did not hit him again until just before sunset.

He blocked the tiller and reached under the stern for the club. It was an oar handle[1] from a broken oar.

The two sharks closed together and as he saw the one nearest him open his jaws and sink them into the silver side of the fish, he raised the club high and brought it down heavy on the top of the shark's broad[2] head.

He struck[3] the shark once more hard across the point of the nose as he slid down[4] from the fish.

The other shark now came in again with his jaws wide[5]. The old man could see pieces of the meat of the fish spilling[6] white from the corner of his jaws.

He swung at him and hit only the head and the shark looked at him and tore[7] the meat loose[8]. The old man swung the club down on him again.

"Come on, *galano*," the old man said. "Come in again."

1. **handle** [`hændl] (n.) 把手
2. **broad** [brɔːd] (a.) 寬的
3. **strike** [straɪk] (v.) 攻擊
   (strike-struck-struck/stricken)
4. **slide down** 往下滑
5. **with one's jaws wide** 張大嘴
6. **spill** [spɪl] (v.) 溢出
7. **tear** [ter] (v.) 撕裂；扯破
   (tear-tore-torn)
8. **loose** [luːs] (a.) 鬆散的

The shark came in and the old man hit him as he shut[1] his jaws. He hit him solidly[2] and from as high up as he could raise the club. This time he felt the bone[3] at the base[4] of the brain and he hit him again in the same place. The old man watched but neither shark returned.

He did not want to look at the fish. He knew that half of him had been destroyed. The sun had gone down while he had been fighting the sharks.

"It will be dark soon," he said. "Then I should see the glow[5] of Havana. If I am too far to the east I will see the lights of one of the new beaches."

1. **shut** [ʃʌt] (v.) 閉上；關上 (shut-shut-shut)
2. **solidly** [ˋsɑ:lɪdli] (adv.) 極用力地
3. **bone** [boʊn] (n.) 骨頭
4. **base** [beɪs] (n.) 底部；根部
5. **glow** [gloʊ] (n.) 光輝；發光
6. **ruin** [ˋru:ɪn] (v.) 毀壞
7. **something comes into one's head** 突然想到某事
8. **spear** [spɪr] (n.) 似矛的東西（在此指魚的嘴巴）
9. **have the luck to . . .** 夠幸運能夠……
10. **forward** [ˋfɔːrwərd] (a.) 前面的
11. **violate** [ˋvaɪəleɪt] (v.) 破壞

He could not talk to the fish anymore because the fish had been ruined[6] too badly. Then something came into his head[7].

"Half-fish," he said. "Fish that you were. I am sorry that I went too far out. I ruined us both. But we have killed many sharks, you and I, and ruined many others. How many did you ever kill, old fish? You do not have that spear[8] on your head for nothing."

I have half of him, he thought. Maybe I'll have the luck to[9] bring the forward[10] half in. I should have some luck.

"No," he said. "You violated[11] your luck when you went too far outside."

"Don't be silly," he said aloud. "You may have much luck yet. I'd like to buy some if there were any place they sell it," he said.

What could I buy it with? he asked himself. Could I buy it with a lost harpoon and a broken knife and two bad hands?

"You might," he said. "You tried to buy it with eighty-four days at sea. They nearly sold it to you too."

He saw the reflected[1] glare[2] of the lights of the city at what must have been around ten o'clock at night. He steered[3] inside of the glow and he thought that now, soon, he must hit the edge[4] of the stream[5].

Now it is over, he thought. They will probably hit me again. But what can a man do against them in the dark without a weapon?

I hope I do not have to fight again, he thought.

1. **reflected** [rɪ`flektɪd]
   (a.) 反射的
2. **glare** [gler] (n.) 耀眼的光線
3. **steer** [stɪr] (v.) 掌舵；行進
4. **edge** [edʒ] (n.) 邊緣
5. **stream** [stri:m] (n.) 潮流
6. **useless** [`ju:sləs]
   (a.) 無作用的
7. **in a pack** 一群
8. **desperately** [`despərətli]
   (adv.) 絕望地；孤注一擲地
9. **seize** [si:z] (v.) 攫住；抓住
10. **be gone** 不見；消失
11. **rudder** [`rʌdər] (n.) 船舵

But by midnight he fought and this time he knew the fight was useless[6]. They came in a pack[7]. He clubbed desperately[8] at what he could only feel and hear and he felt something seize[9] the club and it was gone[10].

He jerked the tiller free from the rudder[11] and beat and chopped with it holding it in both hands and driving it down again and again.

One came, finally, against the head itself and he knew that it was over. He swung the tiller across the shark's head. He swung it once and twice and again. The shark let go[1] and rolled away. That was the last shark of the pack that came. There was nothing more for them to eat.

The old man could hardly breathe now and he felt a strange taste in his mouth. It was coppery[2] and sweet and he was afraid of[3] it for a moment. He spat[4] into the ocean and said, "Eat that, *galanos*."

He knew he was beaten now finally and without remedy[5]. He put the sack around his shoulders and put the skiff on her course. He had no thoughts nor any feelings of any kind. He only noticed[6] how lightly and how well the skiff sailed now that there was no great weight beside her.

He could feel he was inside the current now and he could see the lights of the beach along[7] the shore.

1. **let go** 放棄;放手
2. **coppery** [ˋkɑːpəri] (a.) 銅的
3. **be afraid of** 恐懼;擔心
4. **spit** [spɪt] (v.) 吐(唾液等)
   (spit-spat-spat)
5. **remedy** [ˋrɛmədi] (n.) 補救
6. **notice** [ˋnoʊtɪs] (v.) 注意到
7. **along** [əˋlɔːŋ] (prep.) 沿著

When he sailed into the little harbor the lights of the Terrace were out and he knew everyone was in bed[1].

He pulled the boat up[2] and then he stepped out and tied her to a rock. He took the mast[3] out of its step and furled[4] the sail and tied it. Then he put the mast on his shoulder and started to climb. It was then that he knew the depth of his tiredness[5].

He stopped and looked back and saw the white naked line of the fish's backbone[6] and the dark mass[7] of the head with the bill[8] and all the nakedness[9] in between[10].

He started to climb again and at the top he fell and lay for some time[11] with the mast across his shoulder. He tried to get up. But it was too difficult and he sat there with the mast on his shoulder.

1. **be in bed** 睡覺
2. **pull up** 停下
3. **mast** [mæst] (n.) 船桅
4. **furl** [fɜːrl] (v.) 捲起；收起
5. **tiredness** [`taɪərdnəs] (n.) 疲倦

6. **backbone** [`bækboʊn] (n.) 脊骨
7. **mass** [mæs] (n.) 大塊；大片
8. **bill** [bɪl] (n.) 喙
9. **nakedness** [`neɪkɪdnəs] (n.) 赤裸
10. **in between** 中間

Finally he put the mast down and stood up.

He picked the mast up and put it on his shoulder and started up the road. He had to sit down five times before he reached his shack.

Inside the shack he leaned the mast against the wall[12]. In the dark he found a water bottle and took a drink. Then he lay down on the bed. He pulled the blanket over his body[13] and he slept face down on the newspapers with his arms out straight and the palms[14] of his hands up.

He was asleep when the boy looked in the door in the morning. The boy saw the old man's hands and he started to cry. He went out very quietly to get some coffee and all the way down the road he was crying.

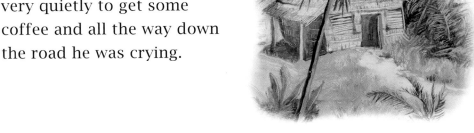

11. **for some time** 一小段時間
12. **lean A against the wall** 把 A 靠在牆上
13. **pull the blanket over one's body** 拉條毯子蓋在身上
14. **palm** [pɑːm] (n.) 手心

Many fishermen were around the skiff looking at what was lashed beside it and one was in the water, his trousers rolled up[1], measuring[2] the skeleton[3].

The boy did not go down. He had been there before and one of the fishermen was looking after[4] the skiff for him.

1. **roll up** 捲起來
2. **measure** [`mɛʒər]
   (v.) 測量
3. **skeleton** [`skelɪtn] (n.) 骸骨
4. **look after** 看顧
5. **disturb** [dɪ`stɜ:rb] (v.) 打擾

"How is he?" one of the fishermen shouted.

"Sleeping," the boy called. He did not care that they saw him crying. "Let no one disturb[5] him."

"He was eighteen feet from nose to tail," the fisherman who was measuring him called.

"I believe it," the boy said.

He went into the Terrace and asked for[6] a can of coffee.

"Hot and with plenty of milk and sugar in it."

"Anything more?"

"No. Afterwards[7] I will see what he can eat."

"What a fish it was," the proprietor[8] said. "There has never been such a fish. Tell him how sorry I am."

"Thanks," the boy said.

6. **ask for** 要求
7. **afterwards** [ˈæftərwərdz] (adv.) 之後

8. **proprietor** [prəˈpraɪətər] (n.) 經營者；所有人

🎧 54

The boy carried the hot can of coffee up to the old man's shack and sat by[1] him until he woke. Finally the old man woke.

"Don't sit up[2]," the boy said. "Drink this."

He poured[3] some of the coffee in a glass.

The old man took it and drank it.

"They beat me, Manolin," he said. "They truly beat me."

"He didn't beat you. Not the fish."

"No. Truly. It was afterwards."

"Pedrico is looking after the skiff and the gear[4]. What do you want done with the head?"

"Let Pedrico chop it up[5] to use in fish traps[6]."

1. **sit by** 坐在……旁邊
2. **sit up** 坐起身子
3. **pour** [pɔːr] (v.) 倒；灌
4. **gear** [gɪr] (n.) 工具
5. **chop up** 切碎
6. **trap** [træp] (n.) 陷阱
7. **spear** [spɪr] (n.) 矛；似矛的東西（此處指魚嘴）
8. **keep** [kiːp] (v.) 留著 (keep-kept-kept)
9. **search for** 搜尋；尋找
10. **coast guard** 海岸巡邏隊

"And the spear[7]?"

"You keep[8] it if you want it."

"I want it," the boy said. "Now we must make our plans about the other things."

"Did they search for[9] me?"

"Of course. With coast guard[10] and with planes."

"The ocean is very big and a skiff is small and hard to see," the old man said. He noticed how pleasant it was to have someone to talk to instead of[1] speaking only to himself and to the sea.

"I missed you," he said. "What did you catch?"

"One the first day. One the second and two the third."

"Very good."

"Now we can fish together again."

"No, I am not lucky, I am not lucky anymore."

"The hell[2] with luck," the boy said, "I'll bring the luck with me."

"What will your family say?"

1. instead of 而不是
2. hell [hɛl] (int.)
    （咒罵語）該死；混蛋
3. have much to learn
    還有很多要學
4. chest [tʃɛst] (n.) 胸膛

"I do not care. I caught two yesterday. But we will fish together now for I still have much to learn[3]. You get your hands well, old man."

"I know how to care for them. In the night I spat something strange and felt something in my chest[4] was broken."

"Get that well too," the boy said. "Lie down, old man. I will bring you your clean shirt. And something to eat."

"Bring any of the papers of the time that I was gone," the old man said.

"You must get well[1] fast for there is much that I can learn and you can teach me everything. How much did you suffer?"

"Plenty," the old man said.

"I'll bring the food and the papers," the boy said. "Rest well, old man. I will bring something from the drugstore[2] for your hands."

As the boy went out the door and down the road he was crying again.

That afternoon there was a party of[3] tourists at the Terrace, and looking down in the water among the empty beer cans and dead barracudas[4] a woman saw a great long white spine[5] with a huge tail at the end that lifted and swung with the tide[6].

1. **get well** 恢復健康
2. **drugstore** [`drʌgstɔːr] (n.) 藥局
3. **a party of . . .** 一群（人）
4. **barracuda** [ˌbærəˋkuːdə] (n.) 梭魚
5. **spine** [spaɪn] (n.) 脊椎
6. **tide** [taɪd] (n.) 潮汐；浪潮
7. **eshark = a shark** 一隻鯊魚
8. **form** [fɔːrm] (v.) 構造；成形
9. **companion** [kəmˋpaniən] (n.) 伙伴；同伴
10. **sleep on one's face** 臉朝下睡覺

"What's that?" she asked a waiter and pointed to the long backbone of the great fish that was now just garbage waiting to go out with the tide.

"*Tiburon*," the waiter said, "Eshark[7]." He wanted to explain what had happened.

"I didn't know sharks had such handsome, beautifully formed[8] tails."

"I didn't either," her male companion[9] said.

Up the road, in his shack, the old man was sleeping again. He was still sleeping on his face[10] and the boy was sitting by him watching him. The old man was dreaming about the lions.

A True or False.

T F **1** The old man killed the fish with a harpoon.

T F **2** The big fish was 20 feet long from nose to tail.

T F **3** While the old man was gone, the boy caught four fish.

T F **4** No one searched for the old man while he was gone.

T F **5** The other fishermen felt very sorry for the old man.

B Fill in the blanks with the given words.

> harbor   violated   pack   jaws   swallowed

1 The old man _____ his luck by going too far out to sea.

2 The sharks _____ large parts of the fish with each bite.

3 The old man tried to get back to the _____ with his fish.

4 During the night, the sharks attacked in a _____.

5 The _____ of a shark are terrible.

C Choose the correct answer.

1 What did the boy want to do now that the old man was back?

(a) He wanted to fix dinner for the old man.

(b) He wanted to go fishing with the old man.

(c) He wanted the newspaper to write a story about the old man.

(d) He wanted to go to a baseball game with the old man.

2 What happened to the old man during the last night in the sea?

(a) The old man fell asleep.

(b) The lights of Havana scared the sharks away.

(c) The other fishermen found the old man.

(d) A pack of sharks attacked the old man.

D Match.

1 Mako shark •

2 *galano* shark •

3 shovel-nose shark •

• **a** attacked in a pair, bad-smelling, hunters and scavengers

• **b** fast, beautiful except for its long, finger-like teeth

• **c** like a pig with a mouth wide enough for a person's head

以下為《老人與海》各章節的前半部。一開始若能聽清楚發音，之後就沒有聽力的負擔。先聽過摘錄的章節，之後再反覆聆聽括弧內單字的發音，並仔細閱讀各種發音的說明。以下都是以英語的典型發音為基礎，所做的簡易說明，即使這裡未提到的發音，也可以配合音檔反覆聆聽，如此一來聽力必能更上層樓。

Chapter One pages 14–15　🎧 57

He (**1**) ( ) ( ) ( ) who fished alone in a skiff in the Gulf Stream and he had gone (**2**) days without catching a fish. During the first forty days (**3**) ( ) ( ) the boy's parents had told him that the old man was now (**4**) *salao* – the worst form of unlucky. The boy's parents had ordered him to go in another boat which caught three good fish the first week. It made the boy sad to see the old man come back each day with (**5**) ( ) empty. He always (**6**) ( ) to help him carry the lines, or the gaff and harpoon and the sail patched with flour sacks, so that when it was furled, it looked like the flag of permanent defeat.

❶ **was an old man:** was 的 -s 和其後的 an 連接，聽起來就像是 wasn 的連音；old 和 man 連在一起唸時，old 的 [d] 音會迅速略過，聽起來像是沒有發音。

❷ **eighty-four:** eighty 的 -t- 因前後皆為有聲母音，因此會發出類似 [d] 的有聲子音，在口語或對話時需特別注意發音；對許多英語學習者而言，eighty 和 eighteen 的發音也常常被搞混，但是可以重音的位置來判斷，eighty 的重音在第一音節，eighteen 的重音在第二音節，且 -teen 發音 [ti:n]，可以此分辨兩者。

❸ **without a fish:** without 的重音在 -out 的部分，因此字首 wi- 發音相當微弱，但是若要特別強調「沒有」時，without a fish 每個音節都要清楚發音。

❹ **definitely:** definitely 在本句中為強調用語，重音放在第一音節，至於 -t- 與後面的 -ly 連在一起發音時，[t] 音會極不明顯，聽起來像沒有發音。

❺ **his skiff:** his 和 skiff 相連，兩個 s 只發音一次，當相同的音連在一起，就不會各自單獨發音。

❻ **went down:** went 的 -t 與 down 連在一起發音時，[t] 會省略不發音，此為美語發音的特徵。

The old man was thin and gaunt (❶) (   ) (   ) on the back of his neck and deep scars on his hands from handling lines of heavy fish.

The (❷) (   ) (   ) the benign skin cancer that the tropical sun brings were on his cheeks. His scars were as old as forgotten memories.

Everything about him was old (❸) (   ) (   ). They were the same color as the sea and were cheerful and undefeated.

"Santiago," the boy said to him, "(❹) (   ) (   ) (   ) (   ) again. We've made some money." The old man had taught the boy to fish and the boy loved him.

"No," the old man said. "You're with a lucky boat. (❺) (   )."

"But remember how you went eighty-seven days without fish and then we caught big ones every day for three weeks."

"I remember," the old man said. "I know you (❻) (   ) (   ) me because you doubted."

❶ **with deep wrinkles:** 重音放在 deep 這個字，with 的 -th 發 [ð] 音，但在不強調時往往不會清楚地發出該音，故聽起來就像 wi 的音，可由前後文判斷正確的單字。

❷ **dark spots of:** dark 的 -k 與 spot 連在一起時，[k] 的發音會迅速略過，重音放在 spots 上，而 spots 和 of 連在一起時，of 會變化成 a 的輕音，並與 spots 形成連音。

❸ **except his eyes:** except 和 his 連在一起時，his 的 [h] 音消失變成連音，通常以 h 開頭的代名詞（如 he、him、his、her）或助動詞（如 have、had 等），在發弱音時，[h] 音會略過聽不見。

❹ **I could go with you:** could 以及發音類似的助動詞 should、would 等，字尾的 [d] 音通常發很輕的音，必須仔細專注才能聽得見。

❺ **Stay there:** stay 的 -t- 發有聲子音，通常 s 後面若緊接著 [p]、[t]、[k] 等音，就會出現接近沒有氣音的有聲子音。

❻ **did not leave:** did 與 not 連在一起發音時，第二個 [d] 音會省略，與 not 一起發連音。

Listening Comprehension

🎧 59 **A** True or False.

T F ❶
_____

T F ❷
_____

T F ❸
_____

T F ❹
_____

T F ❺
_____

T F ❻
_____

🎧 60 **B** Listen to the CD and choose the correct answer.

❶ _____?

    (a) How to catch a big fish.

    (b) How an old man overcame an unlucky streak.

    (c) How an old man proves that he can still catch fish.

❷ _____?

    (a) He won a very long arm-wrestling match.

    (b) He was a great baseball player.

    (c) He always caught the biggest fish.

61 C Listen to the CD and fill in the blanks.

1. It made the boy sad to see the old man come back each day with his _____ _____.

2. There was no cast net, but they went _____ _____ _____ every day.

3. He was _____ _____ and it was no effort for him.

4. He is a great fish but I must _____ him that he is _____ _____ for me.

5. If you do not sleep you might become _____ in the head.

6. The old man felt _____ _____ _____ and he could not see well.

62 D Listen to the CD and write down the sentences. Rearrange the sentences in chronological order.

1. _____

2. _____

3. _____

4. _____

5. _____

_____ ⇨ _____ ⇨ _____ ⇨ _____ ⇨ _____

143

海明威

（Ernest Hemingway, 1899–1961）

　　歐內斯特・海明威是來自伊利諾伊州的美國小說家。他最早的作品是篇刊登於高中校報的短篇小說，並在其中展現了說故事的才華。高中畢業後，他決定不上大學，在當地報社擔任記者。

　　1918 年，海明威加入紅十字會，參與了第一次世界大戰。他在義大利前線受傷後便返國，隨後他前往歐洲當外國記者，於此期間與許多名作家交流，並持續寫作。

　　1923 年，他的第一本書《三個故事和十首詩》（*Three Short Stories and Ten Poems*）出版。1929 年的《戰地春夢》（*A Farewell to Arms*）則是為他奠定小說家名聲的重要著作。1952 年出版的《老人與海》（*The Old Man and the Sea*）描述了老漁夫為捕捉大魚的孤獨奮鬥，廣獲好評，此書也獲頒 1953 年普立茲獎與 1954 年諾貝爾文學獎。

　　海明威於 1961 年 7 月死於槍傷，後被認作自殺。海明威被視為 20 世紀最偉大的作家。

　　《老人與海》說明了海明威所崇尚、描述與追求的生命精神。故事講述一位老漁夫，在數週一無所獲後，終於捕捉到一尾大旗魚。但是他帶著魚返家途中，魚肉被鯊魚食盡，當他抵達港灣時，只徒剩一副魚骨。

　　這簡單故事情節不含任何偉大的象徵或哲學。海明威只是用老人從不停歇的奮鬥故事，生動描繪一段經歷執著痛苦、終獲歡喜勝利的戰役。

　　如同老人在書中所言：「一個人可以被毀滅，但決不能被擊敗。」老人出於本性想盡辦法保住上鉤的大旗魚，他堅苦卓絕的努力，訴說了人類精神的永恆勝利，來自其不屈不撓的勇氣，這也是海明威理念的呈現。

　　海明威用簡單卻強勁的文字，描述漁人精神與生命動力。《老人與海》被譽為海明威信念的最佳體現：雖然生命是場戰鬥，失敗最終無可避免，但奮鬥的過程本身即是值得尊敬的勝利，同時也將替人贏得了尊嚴。

145

p. 12 老人

我一生以捕魚為業，我現在年紀很大了，但是身體依然硬朗，意志也很堅決。我非常精通捕魚，這也代表我有很豐富的捕魚知識，但是最近我已經好幾個星期沒有魚獲了，我知道我很快就會再捕到魚，所以我每天乘船出海垂釣。

男孩

我住在哈瓦那，離其他漁民居住的海灘很近。我很小的時候就學會捕魚，老人教會我捕魚的一切知識。他是個很棒的人，但我父母卻認為他是個不祥之人。我相信他有一天終會再捕到大魚。

p. 14–15

[第一章] 極度的厄運

　　他是一名駕著小船獨自在墨西哥灣流中捕魚的老人，他已經連續八十四天毫無漁獲了。在前面四十天都無漁獲時，小男孩的父母告訴他，老人現在無疑就是 *salao*，意思是運氣背到極點。男孩父母要他跟著另一艘船出海，那艘船出海第一週就捕到三條上等的大魚。

　　看著老人每天駕著空蕩蕩的小艇回航，男孩很難過，他總是會過去幫忙老人扛起魚線、搭鉤、魚叉等魚具，以及滿是麵粉袋補丁的船帆，帆收捲起來時，看起來活像一面象徵注定失敗的旗幟。

　　老人的身形清癯瘦削，頸部後方有一道道深烙的皺紋，雙手也因捕到大魚時拉扯魚線，留下了一條條深深的疤痕。

他的臉頰上布滿深色斑點，那是熱帶地區的炙熱陽光造成的良性皮膚腫瘤。他雙手上的舊疤當時是怎麼留下來的，已不復記憶。

他身上的一切都是蒼老的，除了那一雙眼睛。他的雙眼湛藍如海，神采奕奕，一副不屈不撓的樣子。

p. 16–17 「聖地牙哥，」 男孩對老人說：「我可以再跟你一起出海，以前我們也一起賺了些錢的。」

老人過去教導男孩捕魚，小男孩非常敬愛他。

「不，」老人說，「你跟了一艘幸運的漁船，繼續待在那兒吧。」

「但是你還記得嗎？那時候你連續八十七天都沒捕到魚，接下來的三個星期，我們每天都捕到了大魚。」

「我記得。」老人說，「我知道你不是不信任我的技術才離開的。」

「是爸爸叫我去的，我只是個小孩，我得聽他的。」

「我明白。」老人說。「他的信心不夠。」

「沒錯，但是我們有信心吧？」

「沒錯。我可以先請你去露臺酒館喝杯啤酒，然後再把這些工具搬回家嗎？」

「當然好啊！」老人說，「漁夫之間的小酌。」

p. 18–19 他們坐在露臺酒館裡，許多漁夫取笑老人，但老人並不以為意。年紀大一點的漁夫看著老人，心裡為他感到難過，但是都沒有表露出出來。

那天大豐收的漁夫們都已經把旗魚切好，準備搬上放滿冰塊的卡車，運回哈瓦那市場去。至於那些捕到鯊魚的漁夫，則把鯊魚運到海灣另一邊的鯊魚工廠去。當風自東方吹來，也從鯊魚工廠帶來一陣魚腥味。

　　「聖地牙哥。」男孩喊道。

　　「嗯？」老人回答，他心中浮現多年前的回憶。

　　「我能不能去幫你準備些明天要用來當餌的沙丁魚？」

　　「不行，你去打棒球吧！我還有力氣划船，羅傑利會幫我撒網。」

　　「我想要幫你做，就算我不能和你一起捕魚，也希望能幫點忙。」

　　「你已經請我喝啤酒了啊！」老人說道：「你現在是個大人了！」

　　「我第一次和你一起上船的時候幾歲？」

　　「五歲，我太早把一隻魚拖上船，差點害你丟了小命，船也幾乎給毀了，你還記得嗎？」

p. 20–21　「我還記得那條魚的尾巴甩個不停，還有那陣拍打的聲音。」

　　「你真的記得嗎？」

　　「我記得我們一起捕魚的每一件事。」

　　老人看著他，眼神充滿驕傲與慈祥，「如果你是我的孩子，我會帶你一起出海，」他說，「但是你是你父母的孩子，而且你現在跟的船正在走運。」

　　「那我能幫你準備些沙丁魚嗎？我還知道哪裡能找到四種魚餌。」

　　「我今天還有剩下一些。」

「我去幫你準備四個新鮮的魚餌。」

「一個就夠了。」老人說道，他一直都深具希望與信心的。

「兩個。」男孩說。

「那就兩個吧。」老人同意了，「你不是偷來的吧？」

「我是可以偷，」男孩說，「不過這些是我買的。」

「謝謝，」老人說，「由這股潮流來看，明天應該會是豐收的一天。」

他的想法太單純，壓根沒想過自己何時該學會謙遜。

不過他深知，即使擁有驕傲自信也沒什麼損失。

「你明天要去哪裡？」男孩問。

「很遠，我想要在天亮前就出海。」

p. 22–23 「你現在還有力氣捕真的很大的魚嗎？」

「可以吧，我懂得很多技巧。」

「我們把這些工具拿回家吧。」男孩說，「我可以去拿漁網捕些沙丁魚。」

他們拾起船上的用具。

老人把船杆扛在肩上，男孩拿起裝著各種捕魚工具的木箱。

他們一起走到老人的小屋，穿過敞開的大門。小屋是用被叫作 *quano* 的大王椰子樹的最堅硬部分所建造的。

小屋裡有一張床、一張桌子、一張椅子，在滿是灰塵的地板上，有個角落用來燒炭煮東西。在棕褐色的牆上，掛著一幅彩色的耶穌聖心像以及一幅科比瑞聖母圖，兩樣都是老人妻子的遺物。

過去牆上原還掛著他妻子的照片，但後來老人把它拿了下來，因為那照片總讓他備感孤寂，現在收在角落架子裡，擺在他洗乾淨的襯衫底下。

p. 24–25 「你要吃什麼？」男孩問。

　　「一鍋黃米飯配魚吃，你要不要也來一點？」

　　「不用了，我等一下要回家吃飯，要我幫你生個火嗎？」

　　「沒關係，我等一下自己弄就好。」

　　「我可以拿漁網嗎？」

　　「當然可以。」

　　男孩知道老人家裡根本就沒有漁網，他還記得漁網是什麼時候被賣掉的，但他們每天就這麼假裝演戲，當然也沒有那一鍋黃米飯和魚，男孩心知肚明。

　　「85 是個幸運數字。」老人說，「要是我捕到一條超過千磅重的大魚回來，你應該會很高興吧？」

　　「我去拿網捕些沙丁魚，你要坐在門口曬曬太陽嗎？」

　　「好啊，我有昨天的報紙，我要來看看棒球的消息。」

　　男孩不知道他是不是真有昨天的報紙，不過老人真的從床鋪底下拿出來了。

　　「培利戈在酒館拿給我的。」老人解釋道。

　　「我捕到沙丁魚就回來，我會把你的那一份和我的一起擺在冰上，明天早上我們可以一起用，等我回來你也可以跟我說些棒球的消息。現在記得要保暖啊，老先生，現在已經是九月分了呢。」男孩說。

　　「是上等魚貨出現的月分，」老人說，「而在五月，誰都有能耐當漁夫。」

　　「我要去捕沙丁魚了。」男孩說。

p. 26–27 男孩回來的時候，老人已經在椅子上睡著，太陽也已經下山了。

男孩從床上拿下破舊的軍毯，鋪在椅背上，讓它覆蓋著老人形狀奇特但有力的肩膀上。

他的襯衫已經補丁太多次，看起來就像一張帆，老人的臉十分蒼老，閉起眼睛時似乎毫無血色，兩隻腳打著赤腳。

男孩沒有吵醒老人，等他再回來，老人依然沉睡。

「醒醒啊，老先生。」男孩説。

老人張開眼睛，他神情恍惚一會兒才清醒過來。

之後他笑了。

「你捕到些什麼？」他問道。

「晚餐，」男孩説，「我們來吃晚餐吧。」

「我不怎麼餓。」

「來吃一些吧，你不能光捕魚不吃飯。」

「我們今天吃什麼？」

「有黑豆、白飯、炸香蕉和一些燉菜。」

p. 28–29 這些食物是男孩從露臺酒館的鍋裡拿的。

「你真是好心，」老人説，「我們來吃吧！」

「我就是要叫你來吃飯的，」男孩輕聲地跟他説道，「我想等你要吃的時候再把蓋子打開。」

「我要吃了，」老人説，「只是我得先洗個手。」

「他要去哪兒洗啊？」男孩想。村裡供應的水在兩條街外，我應該幫他提些水過來，還有香皂、毛巾。我怎麼會這麼粗心呢？我還得幫他準備另一件襯衫和夾克在冬天禦寒，再準備一些鞋子和另一條毯子。

「你的燉菜味道好極了！」老人說。

「跟我說說棒球的消息。」男孩問他。

「就像我之前說的，美國大聯盟最值得一瞧的就是洋基隊。」老人開心地說道。

「他們今天輸了！」男孩對他說。

「那沒什麼大不了的，偉大的狄馬喬又重振雄風了。」

「他們隊裡還有其他人。」

「是沒錯，但是有他在可就不一樣了。」老人說，「你還記得他以前去過露臺酒館嗎？我本來想邀他去釣魚，不過不好意思開口，後來我叫你去幫我問，你也害羞不敢問。我想帶偉大的狄馬喬去釣魚，聽說他父親也是漁夫，說不定也和我們一樣窮，能夠了解我們的狀況。

我曾經跟過一艘大船上，航行到非洲，傍晚時還在海邊看到了獅子。」

「我知道，你跟我說過。」

p. 30-31 「我們是在討論非洲還是棒球？」

「棒球，跟我說說麥葛洛的事。」男孩說。

「過去那段日子他有時候會出現在露臺酒館，不過他要是一喝太多，言行就會失態。」

「那麼說真的，誰是最棒的經紀人，是魯基還是龔薩雷茲？」

「我覺得他們旗鼓相當。」

「至於最棒的漁夫，就是你。」

「不是，我知道有人比我更好。」

「你怎麼能這麼說？」男孩說道，「許多漁夫可能不錯，或許有一些真的很棒，但你就這麼一個！」

「謝謝你，你這樣說叫我很開心。希望不要來條太大的魚讓我對付不了，免得證明我們錯了。」

「你的力氣要是還像你說的那樣大，那再大的魚也不怕。」

「我可能已經不再像我想的那麼有力氣了，」老人說，「但我懂得很多捕魚的技巧，我還有堅定的決心。」

「你該上床睡覺了，這樣明天早上才會有精神。」

「晚安！我明天早上會叫你起床。」

「你就是我的鬧鐘。」男孩說。

「我的鬧鐘就是我的年紀，」老人說，「為什麼老人家總是一大早就醒？難道是為了醒著活久一點？」

「我不知道，」男孩說，「我只知道年輕人可以睡得很晚很熟。晚安囉，老先生！」

他們吃飯的時候桌上並沒有燈。

老人把他的一條褲子捲起來，把報紙塞在裡面當枕頭，接著他將整個身體蜷縮在毯子下，睡在鋪在彈簧床上的其他舊報紙上面。

p. 32–33

海明威及《老人與海》

在海明威寫《老人與海》時，他自己也已經邁入老年。他的前一本書並非佳作，但是《老人與海》一推出卻空前成功。海明威使用簡潔精鍊的語言來描寫一位老人要成功的決心，再次緊緊抓住舉世許多讀者的心。有些人認為海明威其實是在描寫他自己，想要再一嚐成功作家的滋味。

很多人認為老人一角取材自葛瑞格・富安帝斯，一名為海明威工作的古巴人。在海明威居住於古巴期間，富安帝斯是他所擁有的漁船「Pilar 號」的船長。

不過，富安帝斯曾對記者提出不同的說法，某天他與海明威乘坐在「Pilar 號」時，他們看見一位老漁夫坐在一艘小船上，船緣掛著一條大魚，海明威對富安帝斯說他想要寫關於這個漁夫的故事。

　　這個故事可能是海明威結合自己與朋友的故事，再加上他所見的人物而創作出主角。這也可能是本故事能感動那麼多讀者的原因，因為老人的角色正好反應了那些努力不懈、決心要再獲得成功的人。

p. 34–35

[第二章] 深入遠洋

　　老人在睡夢中見到了兒時的非洲與長長的金色海灘，那時他每晚獨自住在岸邊，在夢裡，他聽見海潮聲，也見到乘浪而返的當地船隻。

　　睡夢中，他嗅到了清晨微風帶來的非洲氣息。

　　他已不再夢見暴風雨，不再夢見女人，不再夢見什麼了不起的大事，也不再夢到大魚、打鬥、和人比力氣這些事，甚至不再夢見亡妻。

　　如今他只夢見那個有獅子的海灘，黃昏時獅子就像小貓一樣中玩耍。他愛這群獅子就如同愛小男孩一般，但是他從未夢見過男孩。

　　現在他醒過來，看著月光下敞開的大門，他把捲起的褲子攤平後穿上，動身去把小男孩叫醒。

　　男孩家的門沒有鎖，老人打開門靜靜走了進去，他輕輕抓著男孩的腳，直到男孩醒過來，轉身看著他。

　　老人點點頭，男孩抓起掛在床邊椅子上長褲，坐在床上穿起來。

p. 36–37 老人走出門口，男孩在後面跟著他，他還是很想睡，老人搭著他的肩膀說道：「我很抱歉。」

「說什麼啦，」男孩說：「這本來就是男人的工作。」

他們走向老人的小屋，在昏暗的天色下，兩個光著腳的男人沿著路走，扛著自己船上的桅杆。

他們到了老人的小屋後，男孩從籃子裡拿出成捲的繩索、魚叉和搭鉤，老人則肩扛船桅和捲起的船帆。

「你要喝點咖啡嗎？」男孩問。

「我們先把工具放到船上，再去喝點咖啡。」

他們來到一個清晨供應漁民餐點的地方，喝了些加了濃縮牛奶的咖啡。

「你睡得好嗎，老先生？」男孩問。他雖然還是有點想睡，但是他現在已經完全清醒。

p. 38–39 「非常好，瑪諾里，」老人說，「我今天充滿信心。」

「我也是，」男孩說，「現在我該去拿你和我要用的沙丁魚，還有給你新鮮的魚餌。」

「我馬上就回來，」男孩說，「再喝杯咖啡，這裡可以賒帳。」

老人慢慢喝著咖啡，這會是他今天一整天唯一的食物，他知道該把它喝完。長久以來他不熱衷飲食，也從不帶著午餐出海。

他在小船頭邊放了一瓶水，那就是他一整天唯一需要的。

這時男孩帶著沙丁魚和兩個魚餌回來，他們踏上小船，腳下踩著的是帶著石粒的細沙。他們解開纜繩，把小船划向海中。

「祝你好運，老先生。」

「也祝你好運！」老人回道。

他把船槳用繩索固定在船椽的槳架上，身子往前傾，在黑暗中開始划出港口。

除了老人以外，還有其他船隻前進大海，雖然老人看不到他們，但還是可以聽到船槳碰到水面往前推進的聲音。

p. 40–41 老人知道這次他將航向遙遠的外海，土地的氣息他已然拋到腦後，只管划向清晨嶄新的海洋香氣。

老人身處一片黑暗之中，但他可以感覺到白晝即將來臨。划船時，他聽到飛魚躍出水面的聲音。他很喜歡飛魚，牠們是他在大海中最忠實的朋友。

他也很同情飛鳥，特別是那些小巧的黑浮燕鷗，牠們不斷飛行尋找著食物，卻常常一無所獲。

他心想：「鳥兒過著比人類更加辛苦的生活，除了那些搶奪食物和長得又大又壯的飛鳥。為什麼創造出像燕鷗那麼細緻美麗的鳥，卻又讓牠們生活在大海這個嚴苛的環境裡？大海雖然寬廣美麗，但也是非常無情的。」

他總是把大海想成他的「 *la mar* 」，在西班牙文中，這是對愛人的稱呼。那些熱愛大海的人也有時不免數落大海，但在口氣上都把大海當成女人來看待。

一些開著汽艇的年輕漁夫會將大海視為 *el mar*（男性），提到大海時，就把它想成競爭對手甚至是對立的敵人。

但是老人總把大海想成女性，她有時會略施恩惠，有時卻又不假辭色，要是她做了什麼瘋狂或邪惡的事，完全是因為她無法克制自己。他認為月亮的變化盈缺影響著她，一如影響著婦女一樣。

p. 42–43 他平穩地往前划，沒花什麼力氣。

　　「今天我要划到鰹魚和長鰭鮪群聚集處，說不定會有大魚隨著魚群出現。」

　　在天還未大亮之前，他隨著水流，將四個餌分別放在四個不同的深度，魚鉤上的每部分無不讓大魚感覺鮮甜可口。

　　他把男孩給他的兩條新鮮小鮪魚纏在最深的兩條魚線上，另外兩條魚線上則分別勾著大條的金鰺和巴氏若鰺。

　　每一條魚線都和大筆一樣粗，纏繞在一條棍子上，只要有魚拉到或是碰到魚餌，棍子就會往下沉。

　　現在老人緩緩划著小船，讓魚線保持垂直，並維持在適當的深度。淡淡的太陽從海面升起，讓老人能看見其他船隻，低低地挨著水面，離泊岸不遠。

　　他低下頭看著水面，看著筆直落在深水中的魚線，把讓魚線垂得比其他漁夫更直。

　　「我都讓魚線維持精確的垂直度，」他想，「因為只有我完全不能靠運氣捕到魚。」但誰說得準呢？說不定今天正是我的幸運日，畢竟每天都是個嶄新的開始。

　　運氣佳固然不錯，不過我還是寧願把一切做到最準確，那麼當運氣來敲門時，你就已經做好準備了。

　　就在這時，他看見一隻軍艦鳥伸展著長長的黑色翅膀在前方的空中盤旋，急速往海面俯衝，接著又繼續盤旋空中。

p. 44 「牠捕到獵物了，」老人大聲地對自己說道，「牠不光只是看而已。」

「是鬼頭刀，」老人大聲說，「是隻大鬼頭刀。」

老人看著的同時，一條小鮪魚浮出海面，轉了一圈又墜落到水中，接下來一隻隻的鮪魚在魚餌後方高高跳起。

過了一段時間，放在小船尾端的魚線在他腳下被緊緊拉動了。

老人丟下槳，感覺到小鮪魚顫動拉扯魚線的重量，當他將魚線往船上拉時，還能看見水中青綠色的魚背，老人出於仁慈敲了敲牠的頭，接著便把小鮪魚踢到船尾的背陰處。

p. 46–47 「長鰭鮪，」老人大聲說著，「拿來做魚餌太棒了。」

他不記得從何時開始養成了這種自言自語的習慣，大概是小男孩離開他後，不過他也記不得了。

此刻太陽變得炙熱，老人可以感到陽光晒在頸背上，划船時，感覺汗珠就從背上滴落。這時他看到其中一根凸出水面的綠色釣竿猛地往水中一沉 。

「有了！」他說，「有了！」他收回船槳，伸手抓住魚線，用右手大拇指與食指精巧地控制魚線。

魚線再次晃動，這回並不是猛力的拉扯，老人很清楚這代表什麼：水深一百噚處一條旗魚正吃著魚鉤上的沙丁魚。

太棒了！這肯定是條大魚，他心想著。

吃吧，魚兒，快吃吧！這時他先察覺到一陣細微的拉扯，接著是更猛力的拉扯，想必是沙丁魚的頭鉤在魚鉤上，很難把它從鉤子上扯下來，接著魚線便毫無動靜了。

p. 48–49 「來吧！」老人大聲説道，「聞聞看，味道不錯吧？現在快吃吧，等一下還有鮪魚！別客氣，魚兒們，吃吧！」

接著他感覺到一股沉甸甸而不可思議的重量，那是魚的重量。

他先鬆手讓魚線不斷地下沉再下沉，現在，他已做好準備，手中有三綑 240 呎長的魚線預備著，和沉入海中的魚線一樣長。

「再多吃一點，」他説，「好好地吃啊！」

他想，就吃到魚鉤刺穿你的心臟，奪走你命吧，然後乖乖地浮出水面，我好把魚叉一叉而入。你準備好了嗎？這餐吃夠了嗎？

「就是現在！」他大喊一聲，兩手用力收線，拉回了約一碼長的魚線，接著再繼續不斷地拉，使盡手臂的力氣和全身的重量拉著魚線。

但什麼事也沒發生！大魚只管緩緩游開，老人絲毫無法拉動牠一吋。小船繼續慢慢朝西北方駛去，魚群平順地游開，步調緩慢地在平靜的海水裡悠游。

「真希望小男孩在就好了，」老人大聲地説，「現在我竟然被魚拖著跑。我要全力抓住牠，有必要時才放魚線。感謝上帝，牠只是游到其他地方，而不是往下鑽。」

四小時後，大魚繼續拖著小船游向大海，老人仍然緊緊抓住纏繞背上的魚線不放。

p. 52–53

[第三章] 博鬥的開始

老人回頭看，發現陸地已遙不可見。他想，這不礙事，我可以尋著哈瓦那的燈火回去。大魚可能日落前浮上水面，也可能晚上才浮出來。

我沒有抽筋，力氣也還很大，被魚鉤勾住嘴的是牠，不是我，不過能這麼拉扯魚線的魚可不簡單，但願我能親眼看看我的對手是什麼魚，就算只看一眼也行。

大魚一直沒有改變游向，太陽下山後，天氣轉冷，老人把蓋在裝魚餌桶子上的袋子綁在脖子上，覆蓋至背部。魚線繞在他的肩膀上，他小心翼翼把袋子墊在魚線下方。

他想，我對牠無計可施，牠也拿我無可奈何，他想。

有這麼一回，他站起身在船邊小便。他望著星斗，確認前進的方向。現在船移動的速度更慢，哈瓦那的燈火沒那麼強了，他曉得海流應該是把船帶往東方了。

p. 54–55 不知道今天大聯盟棒球賽結果如何，他想。捕魚時要是能聽收音機該有多好。還是想想你現在的正事吧，別做蠢事。

接著他大聲說：「要是小男孩在旁邊幫忙我就好了，看著這條魚。」

他想，到他這把年紀的人是不該孤伶伶的。但這也是不可避免的事。我要記得在鮪魚還沒發臭前吃了牠，保持一點力氣。千萬要記得，早上要吃掉。他對自己說。

到了晚上，兩隻鼠海豚游到小船邊，老人可以聽見牠們在附近翻滾和噴水聲。

「牠們多乖，」他說，「一起嬉戲玩樂，彼此恩愛，就像飛魚一樣，都是我們的好兄弟。」

p. 56–57 接著他開始憐憫起那條他鉤住的大魚。牠很了不起，很不可思議，不知道牠年紀多大了，老人不禁想著。我以前沒捕過這麼強悍的魚，也沒遇過行徑這麼古怪的魚，說不定牠太聰明了，所以沒有跳。牠只要用力一跳，就能要了我的命。

不過這真是一條上等的大魚，要是肉質鮮美的話，可以拿去市場賣。牠像男子漢一樣咬下魚餌，扯著魚線，在搏鬥時毫不驚慌，不曉得牠是早有計畫，還是牠根本就是和我一樣都豁出去了。」

「要是小男孩在這兒就好了。」他大聲地說。他身體靠著船頭，從繞著肩膀的魚線感覺到大魚扯著線的力量。

「我要到無人的地方，把牠揪出來。現在我們同在一條船上，無法得到任何幫助。」

這時大魚突然掀起一陣大浪，老人被拉跌倒，眼睛下方撞出了一個傷口，臉頰流下一點血，但還沒流到下巴就已經凝結乾涸，他走回船頭，靠在木板上休息。

p. 58–59 不知道為什麼突然掀起大浪，他想，應該是魚線滑過牠的背脊，當然牠的背一定不會比我的背更難受，不過就算牠再厲害，也不可能這麼一直拖著小船跑吧。

「魚啊！」他輕柔地大聲說：「我到死都要陪著你。」

太陽升得更高了，老人明白大魚還沒疲倦，只有一個跡象對老人有利，那就是魚線傾斜度顯示大魚游在海中的深度變淺了，那並不表示牠一定會跳起來，雖說也不無可能。

「上帝啊，讓牠跳來吧，」老人說，「我有足夠的魚線應付牠。」

「魚啊，」他說，「我非常愛你、敬佩你，但我一定要在天黑前把你解決掉。」

一隻小鳥從北方朝小船飛來，那是一隻鶯，老人看得出牠非常疲累。鳥飛到老人頭頂上盤旋，接著便停在魚線上休息。

「你年紀多大啦？」老人問小鳥，「這是你的頭次出遠門嗎？」小鳥兒實在太累了，細小的腳爪緊抓住魚線搖來晃去。

「好好休息一下吧，小鳥。」他說，「休息完就出發好好去碰碰運氣，就像其他人、其他鳥兒或是魚一樣。」

p. 60–61 就在這時，小船被大魚拖得突然傾斜，老人跌坐在船頭，要不是放開一點魚線，支撐住自己的身體，他早已經被拖下船了。

小鳥嚇得飛走了，他仔細摸索右手握著的魚線，發現手正在流血。他把線的重量轉移到左肩上，小心翼翼地跪下，用海水清洗手。

傷口的位置正好是他工作所需要用到的部位，他明白在這場戰役還沒結束前，他必須用到雙手，在一切戰爭開始前他可不願意再弄傷手。

「現在，」他說，「我要吃掉那條小鮪魚。」

他跪下拿出放在船尾的鮪魚，用膝部壓著魚，從鮪魚的脖頸至尾端之間切下幾片深紅色的魚肉。

「看來我吃不完整條魚了。」他說，感覺到魚線穩定和沉重地拉著，這時他的左手抽筋了。

「這算是什麼手？」他說，「要抽筋就抽個夠吧！變成爪子也行，但這對你又有什麼好處？」

他拿起一片魚肉放進嘴裡，慢慢地咀嚼著，味道還可以。

「你感覺怎麼樣啊，我的手？」他問那僵硬如死屍般抽筋的手，「我會替你多吃一點。」

真希望把底下那條魚也餵得飽飽的，他想。牠是我的兄弟，不過我還是得殺了牠，我要保持體力才能辦到。於是他慢慢地把鮪魚片一片片全都吃下肚。

「老天爺幫個忙，讓我不要再抽筋了吧。」他說，「因為不知道這條魚接下來會出什麼招啊。」

他想，牠的計畫到底是什麼？而我又有什麼計畫呢？

p. 62-63 他的左手還在抽筋，但他試著慢慢伸展開來。

我痛恨抽筋，他想，抽筋簡直是和身體作對。接著，他的右手感受到魚線拉扯的方式不一樣了。

「牠要浮上來了」，他說道，「加油啊，左手，加油！」

魚線平穩緩慢地升起，小船前的海面突然升起，大魚浮出水面了。牠不斷地冒出海面，海水從牠的背脊兩側流下著。陽光下，牠閃閃發光，牠的頭和身體兩側呈現出寬條紋的淡紫色。

魚嘴就如棒球棒那麼長，越往前端越尖銳，像一把利劍。牠全身都浮出水面，又俐落地潛入水中，猶如潛水夫。老人看著牠如大鐮刀似的大魚尾落入海裡，魚線也跟著疾速被拉走。

老人說：「牠足足比這條小船還長上兩呎。」他試著用雙手控制著魚線，避免因用力過猛導致魚線斷裂。他心裡明白，要是不能用穩定的拉力減緩大魚的速度，魚可能拉走所有魚線，然後掙脫扯斷。

p. 64–65 他想，這真是條大魚，不過我一定得讓牠服氣，我決不能讓牠發現自己的力量有多大，更不能讓牠知道要是牠快速往前游會有什麼結果。

老人曾經見過許多大魚，也見過不少超過千磅的大魚，甚至一生中曾經捕到過兩條，但都不是在獨自出海的時候。

如今他獨自一人在海上，在看不見陸地的遠洋，他被一條從未見過，甚至從未聽聞過的大魚，牢牢地拴在一起，而他的左手還在抽筋。

不知道牠為什麼要躍出水面？老人納悶，感覺起來，牠跳出來就是要讓我知道牠到底有多龐大，真希望能讓牠看看我是個什麼樣的人，不過這樣牠就會看到我的手在抽筋。

到了中午，老人的手不再抽筋了，感覺舒服了一點，不過還是痛苦，不過他不承認自己的痛苦。

「我沒有信教，」他說，「但是我要誦十遍天主經，十遍聖母經，請保佑我捕到這隻魚，要是讓我抓到牠，我保證一定到科比瑞聖母面前禮拜。上帝啊！我真不知道牠會有這麼大。」

p. 66–67 「不過我一定會解決牠，」他說，「不管牠有多麼偉大。」

他想，雖然這並不公平，但我要讓牠瞧瞧，人類能一個人能做什麼，能有多大的耐力。

「我告訴過小男孩，我是個怪老人。」他說，「現在該是我證明的時候了。」

他想證明這件事上千次了，現在老人又要再證明一次。

「大魚啊，要是你還不累，」他大聲說，「那就太神奇了。」

他現在疲累不堪，努力想些其他的事。他想到了大聯盟，他知道紐約洋基隊正在和底特律老虎隊對打。

今天是比賽的第二天，不知道誰勝誰敗，他想，不過我一定要有信心，我和偉大的狄馬喬一樣，能完美地達成任何目標。

他想，你相信偉大的狄馬喬會像我一樣，和一條魚耗那麼長的時間嗎？我相信他一定會，甚至可以耗更久，因為他年輕又身強力壯，而且他父親也是一位漁夫呢。

p. 68–69

人類與大自然

從人類在洞穴做壁畫的遠古時期開始，藝術作品便一直深受大自然的影響。自人類開始熟悉大自然之後，有時便將其視為競爭對手，或生活所需的供應者。

從人類的歷史來看，自然的力量曾經造成極大的災難，奪走不少人命，不論在陸地或海上，人類都必須不斷奮鬥求生存，而這些奮鬥過程在不同時代便表現在不同的藝術作品中。

例如貝多芬在〈第六號交響曲〉裡表現出雷雨的狂暴劇烈；梅爾維爾的經典文學作品《白鯨記》，細膩地描繪出人與自然間的對抗；至於海明威的《老人與海》一書中，也傳達同樣的主題。

不過從另一個角度來看，海明威書中的老人並不是不斷與自然對抗，自然提供老人生活所需的糧食，即使是一隻迷途的飛鳥，也在老人孤獨的戰役中提供一點陪伴的溫暖。

老人並沒有將自然視為敵人，反而把大海看作頻頻改變心情狀態的女性，有時她溫和而慈愛，有時卻是殘忍又嚴酷。

[第四章] 公平的戰鬥

　　太陽下山了，老人為了增強自己的信心，他回憶起有一次曾在卡薩布蘭加的一間酒館裡，與一名來自古巴西恩富戈斯、人高馬大的黑人比腕力，他可是整個碼頭上最強壯的人。

　　他們的手肘從早到晚都沒離開過桌上那條粉筆畫的線，兩人都極力想把對方的手扳倒在桌上，每隔四小時他們就換裁判，讓別的裁判有時間休息睡覺。

　　一整晚比賽雙方僵持不下，黑人一度只差三吋就能扳倒老人，那時候的老人可不老，而且還是冠軍聖地牙哥。

　　但老人又拼命扳了回來，雖然那黑人不賴，又是個一流的運動員，他有把握絕對可以打敗黑人。到了日出時，黑人的手一次又一次被他壓倒在桌上，直到那隻手無力地垂放在桌上。這場比賽從週日早晨開始，一直到週一早上才告結束。

p. 72–73 很長一段時間，每個人都叫他「冠軍」。之後，他又與人比了幾場，後來就不再和人較勁了。他深信，只要他真的夠有心，他可以打敗任何人，不過他覺得太常用右手，對捕魚不太好。

　　接近天黑時，小船經過一大片如小島般的馬尾藻，這時一隻鬼頭刀咬住他的一小段魚線。老人第一次看見牠躍出水面，在空中瘋狂扭動掙扎。

　　當牠移動至船尾處，老人連忙探出船身，奮力拉起這條帶著紫色斑點的金色光滑的魚。

　　魚的嘴巴抽搐地動著，急促地想擺脫鉤子，運用牠長而扁的身軀，尾巴和頭部拍打船底，一直到老人用船槳敲了牠一下，牠抖了抖身軀，接著便一動也不動。

　　老人看著夕陽落到海中，再看看斜插入海水的粗魚線。

　　「牠完全沒停下來的跡象。」他說。

　　但看著流過手中的海水，他發現大魚的速度稍微慢了下來。

p. 74–75 　「我要把兩支船槳交叉綁在船尾，這樣就可以減緩牠在夜裡游動的速度，」他說，「到了晚上牠會變得更能抵抗，不過我也不弱。」

　　我已經慢慢學會怎麼來對付牠了，他想，至少是學到了這部分。再來，我也記得，大魚自從上鉤後就沒再吃過東西了，這麼大的一條魚，需要更多的食物才夠。而我已經吃了一整條鰹魚，明天我要吃那條鬼頭刀。

　　「現在覺得如何啊，魚兒？」他大聲地問，「我覺得挺不錯的，左手也舒服多了，食物還能撐個一天一夜，繼續拖著船走吧，魚兒。」

　　其實老人並不覺得舒服，因為橫跨在他背部的魚線幾乎讓他痛苦不堪，甚至已經麻木了，這讓他很擔心。

　　不過更糟的我都經歷過了，他想，現在我的手不過被割傷，另一隻手也不抽筋了，腿也沒事。

　　現在天色已暗，時值九月，日落後天黑得快，第一批星星出現了，他叫不出獵戶座「參宿七」的名字，但一看到它，他心裡立刻明白，再過不久其他星星便會冒出頭來，他就可以有這些遙遠的朋友作伴了。

p. 76–77 「這條大魚也是我的朋友，」他大聲地說，「我從沒見過，甚至沒聽過有這麼大的魚，不過我卻得殺了牠，真高興我們不用去捕殺星星。」

接著，他為那條未進食的大魚感到難過，而即使再怎麼同情牠，還是沒有打消把牠解決掉的決心。他想：牠能餵飽多少人啊！但是那些人夠資格享用牠嗎？不，當然不夠格，根本沒有人配吃這麼一條如此尊貴的魚。

老人休息了一段時間，他想大約是兩個小時吧，月亮遲至現在才升起，因此他無從估計時間。現在他的背依然忍受著大魚拉扯前進的魚線。

「但是你到現在都還沒睡過覺呢，老頭子！都已經過了半天又一夜，馬上又是新的一天了，你都完全沒闔過眼。」他大聲說著，「如果魚一直這麼穩定地前進，我得想辦法睡一下，要是再不睡一會兒，腦子可能就不清醒了。」

他對自己說，我是可以不睡覺，不過這太危險了。

他又回到船尾。這時星光閃亮，他能清楚看見那條鬼頭刀，他用刀刺進牠的頭部，施力將牠從船尾拉上來。

鬼頭刀的身體已經冰冷，在星光下顯現銀白色的光芒。老人用右腳踏在魚頭，開始剝去一邊的皮，接著再剝另一側的皮，切下幾塊魚片。他靠近船椽，把手放進水裡，水流變得比較不那麼強了。

「牠累了，也可能在休息，現在我要吃點鬼頭刀，休息一會兒，睡點覺。」

p. 78–79 在星光下，他吃下了一片魚片。

「煮過的鬼頭刀肉可真是美味啊！」他說，「不過生的真是難吃死了！下次沒帶鹽或萊姆我決不上船。」

雲層正往東方天際聚攏，他熟悉的星星一顆顆漸漸消失蹤影，看來他似乎正往一大片雲層前進，風力也漸漸減弱。

「三、四天後天氣會變糟，」他說，「不過今晚和明天還不會變壞，老頭子，趁著大魚平穩前進，現在先打點一下好好睡一覺吧。」

月亮升起好長一段時間了，但老人仍睡著，大魚穩穩地往前拉，小船航向雲層的隧道前進。

老人握著拳頭的右手突然打到臉，他猛然驚醒。握在手中的魚線，讓他的右手掌如烈火灼燒般疼痛，他左手沒有知覺，但他右手極力拉著魚線，魚線卻還是迅速地滑走。

p. 80–81 終於，他左手感覺到魚線的存在。他往後退，用背抵著魚線，現在灼燒的刺痛感從背部蔓延至左手，他的左手承受所有的拉力，所以被魚線割傷得很嚴重。

就在這時，大魚猛然衝出海面，又重重地落下。接下來不斷地躍出海面又遁入海中。即使老人不斷地鬆開魚線，還緊緊拉著以免線被扯斷，但小船依然被拖著急速前進，老人被拖著緊靠在船頭上，臉還碰到切開的鬼頭刀肉片，身體完全不得動彈。

他想，這正是我們期待的，現在就讓我們承擔吧！牠得為賠償這些魚線不可，一定得讓牠付出代價。

老人根本看不到大魚在海面上下跳躍，只聽見牠落水時衝擊與水花飛濺的聲音，魚線滑動的速度太快，把他的雙手割得傷痕累累，但他老早就明白這遲早會發生。

他想，要是男孩也在，他就可以幫忙打濕幾捲魚線，沒錯，要是男孩在該有多好。

魚線不斷被往外拉，不過現在大魚的速度漸漸減緩，老人只能讓線一吋吋被拉走。現在他把頭從木板上抬起，從被臉頰壓爛的魚片上離開。原本他是跪在船上，再慢慢站起身，他仍持續放線，但速度已經慢了下來。

　　p. 82–83 不知道是什麼原因突然驚嚇到牠？是飢餓讓牠感到絕望嗎？還是夜裡的什麼東西嚇到牠了？也許是牠突然感到恐懼？可是牠一向都是這麼鎮定堅強，毫無畏懼又充滿自信，實在是太奇怪了。

　　「你最好也不要害怕，要對自己有信心啊，老頭子。」他說。

　　老人用左手拉著魚線，彎下身用右手舀了點海水，把剛剛被壓在臉上擠爛的鬼頭刀肉給洗掉，他擔心魚肉會讓他反胃，而一嘔吐就會沒體力。

　　他用海水洗淨右手，將手泡在鹹水中，看著日出前的第一道光芒。

　　魚似乎是朝著東方游去，他想，那代表牠已經累了，所以才隨著海流前進，不久牠就會開始打轉，那時我們才要真正開始對決。

　　等他覺得右手泡在水裡差不多了，便把手縮回來瞧一瞧。

　　「還不算太慘，」他說，「對一個男子漢來說，這一點痛根本算不了什麼。」

　　他小心翼翼握著魚線，免得傷口又被魚線割傷。他移動身體重心，以便把手放到船的另一側海水中。

p. 84-85 老人對自己的左手說：「對廢物來說，你還不算一無是處，不過有一陣子，你真讓我洩氣。」

為什麼我與生俱來不是兩隻好手呢？他想，或許是我自己的問題，沒有好好鍛鍊左手，但老天爺知道，它過去學習的機會可不少，況且左手昨晚的表現也並算太差，只有抽筋一次。要是又抽筋的話，就讓魚線把它割斷算了。

自老人出海以來，這已經是第三次日出了，魚才開始在水中繞圈圈。

「牠繞了一大圈，但是至少已經開始打轉了。」他說。

我要儘量抓緊魚線，老人心想，拉力會讓牠繞的圈子越來越小，說不定不到個把鐘頭我就能看到牠浮出水面了，現在我要讓牠心服口服，然後再殺了牠。

但兩小時過去了，那條魚就這麼不疾不徐地地繞著圈，老人渾身已被汗水濕透，累得筋疲力竭。所幸現在大魚繞的圈子小多了，從魚線傾斜度，他可以判斷魚已穩定地往上游。

大約有一小時之久，老人眼前直冒黑點，汗水刺痛他的雙眼及眼睛下方和額頭的傷口；對於眼前那些黑點他並不擔心，但是他卻連續兩次覺得暈眩甚至要昏倒，這反而讓他感到憂心。

p. 86-87 「我不能被打敗，死在這條魚上，」他說，「如今我都把魚這麼漂亮地弄到手了，上帝請幫我熬下去，我會多唸一百遍天主經和聖母經，只是現在我沒辦法唸。」

就當我已經誦過了吧，他想，反正我以後會補唸的。

這時，他感到手中的魚線一陣重重的拉扯，又快又猛。

那條魚在用長喙攻擊魚線，老人心想，牠可能會跳起來，不過現在我寧願牠繼續繞圈子。牠一定要跳起來呼吸新鮮空氣，但是每跳一次，鉤在傷口的裂痕就會加大，反而讓牠能掙脫魚鉤。

「別跳啊，魚兒，」老人說，「千萬別跳！」

大魚又撞擊了魚線好幾次，每次老人都得多放出一些魚線。

過一陣子，魚不再撞擊魚線了，又開始緩慢地兜圈子。老人現在開始緩緩地拉回一些魚線，但他又感覺一陣暈眩，他用左手舀了些海水潑在頭上，又潑了一些水搓揉頸背。

「我沒有抽筋了，」他說，「牠很快就會再浮上來，我一定可以撐住。你一定要撐下去，這還用說嗎？」

這時他背靠船頭跪下來，又再把魚線環繞至背部。

他決定，我要趁著牠繞圈轉時先歇息一會兒，一等牠冒上來，再站起身好好對付牠。

p. 88–89 我從來沒這麼累過，他想，現在已經開始吹起季風了，但要趁風吹起時把牠拖上來。

海水已經隨風漲高，不過今天是微風吹拂的好天氣，而且他還得靠這陣風返航回家呢。

「現在我要往西南方前進，」他說，「人是不會在海上迷路的，況且我住的地方還是個很長的島嶼。」

一直到大魚轉到第三圈時，老人才初次看到牠。起先老人看到船下一抹黑影，花了好久時間才從船底掠過，他簡直不敢相信牠有這麼長。

「不可能，」他說，「牠不可能會這麼大。」

但牠的確就是那麼大，繞完一圈後，牠浮出水面，離小船大約只有三十碼，老人看見牠尾巴露出水面，比大鐮刀的刀鋒還要長，在深藍色的水上呈現淡紫色。

　　大魚就在水面下游著，老人能清楚地看見牠龐大的體積與皮膚上的紫色條紋，牠的背鰭往下彎曲，巨大的胸鰭向外擴張，接著老人見到了牠的眼睛。

　　現在老人汗流浹背，但卻不是因為陽光曬的關係。每當大魚從容地繞完一圈，他就收回一些魚線。他很確定只要大魚再繞兩圈，他就有機會把魚叉刺向牠。

p. 90–91 但是我得想法子讓牠再靠近一點，再近一點，他想，我絕不能刺牠的頭，一定要命中心臟。

　　「老頭子，你要沉著堅強。」他自語說。

　　現在魚繞圈游近小船，從容優雅，只見牠擺動的大尾巴。老人使力把牠拉近一點，這時魚往他這邊斜側了下身，不一會兒，身子又擺直開始繞另一圈。

　　「我拉動牠了！」老人說，「我剛才拖動牠了！」

　　他又感到一陣暈眩，但仍死命地拉住那條魚。

　　我拉動牠了，他想，說不定這次我就能解決掉牠了。

　　手，用力拉啊！他想，腳，站穩啊！頭腦啊，撐下去！為了我，撐下去吧，你從沒暈倒過，這一次我一定要把牠拖過來。」

　　但是就在他使盡全力往前拉時，大魚又調轉方向游走了。

　　「魚啊！」老人說，「魚啊，反正你遲早得死的，難道也要我陪你一起死嗎？」

p. 92-93 這樣下去什麼事也做不了,他想。他口乾得要命,連話都沒辦法說,但是現在又無法伸手拿水來喝。

他心想,這次我一定要把牠拖到船邊,如果牠再多繞幾圈,我可能就沒法好好應付了。

他告訴自己,你可以的,你一直都很行的。

牠在轉下一圈時,他差一點就要把牠拖過來了,可是牠又挺直身子慢慢游開。

老人想,魚啊,你簡直是要我的命啊。不過你絕對有權這麼做。我這輩子還沒見過比你更大、更美、更鎮靜、更高貴的魚了,兄弟。過來殺死我好了,我不管是誰殺了誰。

他想,現在你腦袋都糊塗了,你要保持頭腦清醒,像個男子漢或像魚那樣咬緊牙根。

「清醒一點,腦子。」他用幾乎聽不見的聲音說,「清醒!」

他又試了一次,當他把魚拖轉過來時,覺得自己快暈過去了。而魚又挺直身子,在空中揮動著大尾巴,緩緩游開。

我一定要再試一次,老人對自己發誓,雖然他手早就軟弱無力,眼睛也不好使,只能間歇地看清楚。

p. 96-97

[第五章] 鯊魚攻擊

老人忍受著身上的一切痛苦,用他僅存的力量和久違的的自尊,和魚的痛苦相對抗。

魚游到小船邊,緩緩游著,正要經過小船。

老人把魚線拋下用腳踩著,然後盡量高舉魚叉,使盡全身力氣,一把插進大魚胸鰭的後方。

他感覺到鐵叉刺進魚身,他把身體緊貼著魚叉,使勁把鐵叉刺向更深處,之後再用全身的力量猛推。

隨後大魚突然猛力掙扎，死亡已經降臨在牠身上。牠從水中高高躍起，展露牠驚人的身長與寬度、力量與美麗。牠像是高掛在老人小船的上空，然後又重重地落入水中，激起一大片浪花。

　　p. 98–99 老人覺得暈眩反胃，眼睛也看不清楚，不過他拿掉魚叉上的魚線，讓魚線慢慢滑過滿是傷痕的雙手，當他的視線不再模糊時，他看見大魚翻著銀亮的魚肚浮在水面。

　　魚叉的尖端整個刺穿大魚的肩部，從心臟流出的鮮血染紅了整片海水，魚身銀亮，仍靜靜地隨著海流漂浮，老人把頭埋進雙手裡。

　　「保持頭腦清醒吧！」他說，「雖然我是個疲累的老頭，但還是殺了這條大魚，牠是我兄弟。現在我得開始做辛苦的善後工作。」

　　「我要先把拉繩準備好，把魚綁在小船邊，」他想，「小船根本載不動牠。」

　　老人先把大魚拉到小船邊。我要看看牠，他想，去摸摸牠，感覺牠的存在。

　　如今牠是我的財產了，老人心想，但這不是我想感受牠的原因。我第二次用魚叉刺牠時，似乎感覺到了牠的心跳。現在就把牠拉過來，先用繩索套住魚尾，再用另外一個繩套套住魚身，綁在小船邊。

p. 100–101 「開始幹活吧，老頭子！」老人說，喝了一小口水。

「雖然戰鬥已結束了，但還有很多辛苦的工作要做。」

他抬頭看看天空，又看看他的魚。

「過來吧，魚兒！」他說。但魚並沒有過來，而只是靜靜躺在水面上，老人只好把小船划向牠。

當魚的頭抵到船首時，老人簡直不敢相信牠竟然那麼大。

「要解決牠只有這個辦法。」老人說。現在他覺得舒服多了，頭腦也很清醒。他想，牠一定超過一千五百磅，說不定還更重呢。

「我想偉大的狄馬喬絕對會為我今天的勝利感到驕傲。」

他將大魚緊緊綁在船頭、船尾和中間座板的部分，牠的體積實在太大了，簡直就像是拖了另一艘更大的船在旁一樣。

他可以看到那條魚，而唯有看著他的手，去感覺背部靠著船尾的感覺，他才確定這一切千真確發生過，而不是一場夢。

p. 102 小船和大魚平行綁在一起，共同往前航行，老人心想，就算是牠拉著我走吧，如果這能讓牠高興的話，我唯一勝過牠的不過是比較會要詭計，況且對我沒有惡意。

一個小時後，第一隻鯊魚開始攻擊他。大魚身上一大片暗紅血水沉下擴散到一哩的海水，鯊魚也從海水深處竄上來。

鯊魚竄得很快，整個海面在陽光下濺起一片藍色浪花，接著牠沒入海水中，循著血腥氣味，順著船和魚被拖走的路線游過來。

p. 104–105 有時候鯊魚會追丟這股血腥味，但是牠很快又會找到，然後游得更快更猛。這是一隻很大的灰鯖鯊，是海中游得最快的魚。除了下顎，牠全身都很美。

牠的背部像旗魚一樣藍，魚肚銀亮，外皮光滑美麗。在他下巴緊閉的雙唇內，有八排牙齒全往內傾斜。牠的牙齒不像多數鯊魚一樣呈三角形，牠們彎曲起來像爪子般的牙齒，就像人類的手指，而且有老人的手指那麼長，牙齒兩端有如剃刀般尖利。

老人看見鯊魚游過來時，就知道這是一條無所畏懼、為所欲為的鯊魚。他緊盯著鯊魚接近，準備好魚叉和繩索。

現在老人的頭腦很清醒，雖然意志堅定，但獲勝的機會卻甚為渺茫。

他想，美好的事情總難長久，也許這一切根本就只是一場夢。

我沒辦法阻止牠攻擊我，但我或許能制服牠，你這大牙齒的，老人想，去你媽的真倒楣！

p. 106–107 當鯊魚襲擊大魚時，老人看到牠張開大口，閃著奇特的眼神，就在牠撕扯魚尾肉時，他聽見牙齒的喀嚓聲。

這時他將魚叉猛力刺往鯊魚頭部，再用力推進腦中，他用自己布滿鮮血的雙手對鯊魚展開攻擊，用盡全身的力量把魚叉刺向鯊魚。他擲出魚叉時，心中並不抱任何希望，但下手時卻充滿了決心和全然的敵意。

鯊魚翻了個身，老人發現牠的眼神不再有生氣，他明白牠就快要死了，但牠不願接受這樣的事實。牠在海面上猶如快艇般急速前進，接著動也不動地浮在海面，過了一會兒便緩緩沉入海中。

「牠大概吃掉了我 40 磅的魚肉，還帶走了我的魚叉。」老人說道。他不願再看那條大魚，牠的身體已殘破不全，當鯊魚攻擊牠時，老人感覺就彷彿是自己被攻擊。

美好的事總是那麼短暫，他想，如今真希望這一切只是一場夢，但願我根本就沒釣到那條魚，而是獨自躺在鋪著報紙的床上。」

「但是人不是為失敗而生，」他說，「人可以被毀滅，但決不能被擊敗。」

他想，即便我很難過殺了那條魚，現在艱難的時刻又來臨了，而我連一支魚叉都沒了。

「別想了，老頭子。」他大聲地說著，「還是順著航線往前走吧，無論發生什麼事都要接受。」

p. 108–109 他心裡其實明白得很，等小船划到洋流內會發生什麼事，不過目前還不太需要做什麼準備。

「有辦法了，」他高聲說，「我可以把刀子綁在槳柄上。」

接著他也這麼做了。

「現在，我雖然還是個老頭，但是可不是手無寸鐵。」

他看著魚的前半部身體，又尋回了一線希望。

心中不存希望的人太傻了，他想，而且我相信這絕對是一種罪惡，還是先別想到罪惡吧，眼前的麻煩已經夠多了。

我不懂罪惡，也不確定自己是否相信罪惡。說不定殺魚便是一種罪惡，就算是為了討生活，供魚肉給人吃，也是有罪。這樣說來，每件事都有罪。不要去想這些罪了，你生來就是個漁夫。

你並不僅僅是為了生存賣魚討口飯吃，才殺死那條魚的，他想，你殺牠是因為你是漁夫，你有自尊心。牠活著時你敬愛牠，牠死後你依然如此。如果你敬愛牠，殺了牠就不算罪惡，還是罪更深重？

但是你殺那條大牙齒時卻樂在其中，他想。

「我殺牠是為了自衛，」老人大聲喊著，「我殺牠並沒有不妥。」

況且，他想，一物剋一物，只是方法不同罷了。捕魚能置我於死地，一如捕魚也能養活我一樣。小男孩讓我想活下去，我就別再騙自己了吧。

p. 110–111

加勒比海

若以面積大小來分類，世界上最大的主要海域，分別是南海、地中海與加勒比海。南海常出現在現今的新聞標題中，因為中國、越南、馬來西亞和菲律賓，都想要取得這片海域能源的控制權。

地中海在早期西方文明的演進，扮演極為重要的角色。

最後則是加勒比海，它因澄淨的海水、美麗的珊瑚和豐富的水上活動而馳名，當然也因為海明威的《老人與海》的場景設定在該海域而著名。

喜愛釣魚、潛水，或是想躺在白色沙灘放鬆身心、在清澈海水中游泳的遊客，都將加勒比海視為最佳景點。這裡有許多島嶼過去都是歐洲國家的殖民地。

古巴是其中最大的島嶼，特別的是，它也是現今依然存在的共產國家之一。古巴的首都哈瓦那，也出現在海明威的故事中。這首都曾是著名的觀光景點，是許多美國富豪或名人過去的度假勝地，但自從古巴被社會主義的政府控制後，哈瓦那對遊客已不復往昔的吸引力了。

[第六章] 最後的戰役

老人已經航行兩小時了，他又看見了兩條鯊魚中的第一條。

「鯊魚！」他大喊著。

他拿起纏著刀子的船槳，盡可能不用太大的力氣，因為他的手本能地反抗這股痛苦，他只能看著鯊魚往前逼近。

牠們是兇狠惹人厭的鯊魚，是氣味難聞的清道夫，是無情的殺手。當牠們飢餓時，甚至會一口咬下船槳或是船舵。

「好啊！」老人說，「鯊魚，來吧，鯊魚。」

牠們真的過來了，一隻轉向，游到小船下方不見蹤影，老人感覺小船一陣搖晃。

當鯊魚在猛力拉扯大魚時，另一隻鯊魚用牠黃澄的大眼瞪著老人，接著便火速游向大魚，攻擊牠原本被咬過的部分。

在鯊魚呈棕色的頭上有條清楚的線，一直延伸至後腦與脊髓交界處，老人將綁在船槳上的刀刺向鯊魚的腦袋，把刀抽回來，又再刺向鯊魚如貓一般的黃色雙眼。鯊魚放開口中的大魚，溜進海底，在死前還把先前咬下的魚肉吞下肚裡。

p. 114–115 老人一看到另一隻鯊魚，便傾身對牠猛力一擊，這次猛擊讓他傷了雙手和肩膀，但是鯊魚快速地把頭露出水面，又迅速游了過來，老人毫不遲疑便往牠平坦的頭頂正中心刺下去。

他拔回刀子，再往同一個地方攻擊。接著老人用刀猛刺鯊魚的左眼，但是鯊魚依然不動如山。

「不肯走嗎？」老人說著，把刀刃刺向鯊魚的脊椎骨和腦袋間，他感覺到牠的軟骨被他刺斷了！

「走吧，鯊魚，沉到一哩深海中，去陪伴你的朋友吧！還是說不一定那是你母親？」

老人擦拭著刀鋒，把船槳放下，之後讓小船返回正確的航向。

p. 116–117 「牠們想必吃掉這條大魚的四分之一了，還都是上好的魚肉。」他大聲說道，「真希望這一切只是一場夢，這條大魚根本就沒有上鉤。我心裡很難過，魚兒啊，一切都變調了。」他停頓下來，不願再看大魚一眼。

「我根本就不應該跑來這麼遠的地方，魚啊，」他說，「無論是你或是我，都不應該。我很抱歉，大魚。天知道最後那條鯊魚吃了多少肉，」他繼續說道，「不過小船的確輕了很多，」他根本不敢去想大魚下方到底被咬得多狼狽。

「這條魚大到可以讓人撐一整個冬天，」老人想。「別再想這些了，就休息一下，讓手恢復正常，好好保護你剩下的魚肉吧！」

接下來出現的是一隻單獨行動的鏟鼻鯊。

牠看起來像一隻走近飼料槽的豬，嘴巴大到人都可以把頭伸進去。老人讓牠攻擊大魚，接著用船槳上的尖刀一刀刺向牠的腦袋，但是鯊魚翻了一圈便往後猛退，刀刃也應聲折斷。

大鯊魚緩緩沉入水中，老人甚至不再看一眼。

「我還有個搭鉤，」他說，「不過這用不上，我還有兩支船槳、一把舵柄和一根短棍。」

現在牠們可算打敗我了，他想，我實在太老，沒辦法把鯊魚全給打死，但是只要我還有這有船槳、舵柄和短棍，我就會再拚下去。」

p. 118–119 現在時間已接近傍晚，但是老人眼前除了海洋與天空，其他什麼也看不到。

　　「你累了，老頭子！」他說，「你的內心覺得厭倦了。」日落時，鯊魚又來攻擊老人。

　　他撐住舵柄，跑到船尾下拿出短棍，那原本是斷裂船槳的握柄。

　　兩隻鯊魚同時朝小船逼進，他看見離他比較近的那隻張開血盆大口，上下顎深深陷在大魚銀色的肉上。他高高舉起短棍，往鯊魚寬闊的頭頂奮力敲下。

　　鯊魚從大魚身邊下沉，老人又猛力敲擊牠的鼻尖。

　　這時另一隻鯊魚也張開大口再次進攻，老人見到好幾塊魚肉從牠嘴邊露出。他這次只對著鯊魚的頭部重擊，鯊魚看著他，依然撕扯著魚肉，老人再次揮棍打牠。

　　「來啊，鯊魚，」老人說，「再來啊！」

p. 120–121 鯊魚又衝過來，老人趁牠閉上嘴時再次攻擊，他把棍子盡量舉高，使盡力氣敲向鯊魚，這次他甚至能感覺自己擊中牠的頭底骨，接著便又往同一個地方猛擊。老人繼續警覺地看著，但是再也沒有鯊魚回來攻擊。

　　現在老人根本不想再看大魚一眼，他心裡明白牠已被摧毀了一半，而在他與鯊魚奮戰的同時，太陽也已經下山了。

　　「馬上就要天黑了，」他說，「沒多久我就會看見哈瓦那的燈火。如果我太偏東，就會看到別的海灘上的燈光。」

現在他無法再跟大魚講話了，因為牠已經被攻擊得體無完膚。接著一個想法閃過他腦中。

　　「你這半隻魚呀，」他說，「你之前還是一條完整的魚，很抱歉我出海太遠，把我們倆都給害慘了，不過我們的確殺了不少鯊魚啊，你和我一起幹掉了不少魚。你以前殺過多少魚啊，老魚？你那張尖利的嘴可不是白長的吧！」

　　現在我還有半條魚，他想，說不定我運氣好，還能把這半條帶回去，我應該還有點運氣吧？」

　　「沒有吧，」他說，「你出海太遠，把運氣都給用完了。」

　　「別傻了，」他高聲地說道，「說不定你還有點運氣，要是有地方在賣好運的話，我可要去買一點。」他說。

p. 122–123 但是我能用什麼來買呢？他問自己，難道我能用弄丟的魚叉、折斷的刀子來買嗎？還是用我這兩隻沒用的手？

　　「說不定你真的可以，」他說，「你在海上待了八十四天就是為了買一點運氣，而他們也差一點就賣給你了。」

　　大約晚上十點左右，他看到了城鎮反射出耀眼的光芒，他朝著亮光駛過去，心中想著，再過不久應該就能抵達小溪邊了。

　　現在一切都過去了，老人心想，牠們可能會再來攻擊，但在這片黑暗中，一個手無寸鐵的人又能怎麼對付牠們呢？

　　真希望我不必再搏鬥了，老人想。

　　但是到了午夜時分，他又和鯊魚搏鬥起來。他知道這將是一次無謂的對抗。

牠們成群結隊而來，他只能絕望地憑感覺和聽聲音地胡亂攻擊，突然間他感覺有什麼東西抓住了棍子，然後棍子就沒了。

　　他用力拿起船舵的舵柄，兩手緊緊握住，一次又一次盲目地敲打攻擊。

p. 124–125 最後，一條鯊魚又再一次逼近大魚頭部，奮力搶食，老人知道一切都已結束。他拿著舵柄揮向鯊魚頭部，一次、一次、又一次。鯊魚終於放開，翻滾著游開。這是鯊魚群的最後一隻，大魚身上再也沒有肉給他們吃了。

　　現在這時幾乎喘不過氣來，嘴裡還有種怪異的味道，像是銅與甜味的混合，他擔心了一下。他朝海裡啐了一口，說著：「吃吧，鯊魚！」

　　現在他知道自己最終依然被擊敗，輸得徹徹底底。他把布袋放在肩上，把小船划向正確的航線。現在他無法思考，也毫無感覺，他只注意到沒有了沉重的負荷，小船航行地多麼輕巧順利。

　　他感覺到目前正順著洋流前進，也已經看見岸邊海灘的燈光。

p. 126–127 當船駛進小港灣裡，露臺酒館的燈光已經熄滅，他知道人們都入睡了。

　　他將小船拉上岸，跨步下船，再把船綁在岩石邊。他把船桅卸下，捲起帆布後綁好，然後將船桅扛在肩上，開始往上爬。直到現在，他才明白自己有多疲累。

　　這時他停下腳步，回過頭看著大魚潔白光滑的背脊、顏色深黑帶著尖喙的頭部，以及中間只剩空殼的骨架。

他又開始往上爬，爬到頂端時跌了一跤，於是便將船桅抵在肩上，躺在地上歇了一會兒。老人想站起身，但實在太困難了，便肩上扛著船桅坐在那兒。

終於，他放下船桅站起來，再拿起船桅扛在肩上，開始往路上走。他一路上又歇了五次才走回到他的小屋。

到了屋裡，他把桅杆放到牆邊。在黑暗中他摸到水瓶喝了些水，便倒到床上。他拉起毯子蓋住身子，趴在鋪著報紙的床上，雙臂打直，手心掌朝上，睡著了。

清晨，小男孩從門外往屋裡看，老人仍在沉睡中。男孩看到老人的雙手時，不禁哭了起來。他悄悄地跑去幫他拿些咖啡，一路上都在哭。

p. 128–129 許多漁夫圍在小船邊，看綁在小船旁的是什麼東西，其中有一人捲起褲管走進水中，正在量魚骨的大小。

小男孩並沒有過去，他之前已經去過了，其中一位漁夫在幫他看著那艘小船。

「他還好嗎？」一位漁夫喊道。

「他在睡覺，」男孩大聲說，他不在乎讓其他人看到他在哭，「別讓人去打擾他。」

「牠從鼻尖到尾巴總共是十八呎長。」剛剛在測量魚骨的漁夫吼道。

「這我相信。」男孩說。

他走進露臺酒館要了一罐咖啡。

「熱咖啡，多加點牛奶和糖。」

「還要別的嗎？」

「不用了，過一會兒我再看看他能吃些什麼。」

「好大的一條魚啊，」酒館老闆説，「過去從沒見過這麼大的魚，幫我跟他説我很抱歉。」

「謝謝。」男孩回道。

p. 130–131 男孩拿著那罐熱咖啡來到老人的小屋，坐在他身邊等他醒過來。終於，老人醒了。

「別坐起來，」男孩説，「先把這個喝了吧。」他在杯裡倒了些咖啡。

老人接過咖啡喝下。

「牠們擊敗我了，瑪諾里，」他説，「牠們完完全全地擊敗我了。」

「沒有，那條魚沒有擊敗你。」

「牠的確沒有打敗我，不過，後來卻把我打敗了。」

「培利戈在幫你看著小船和釣具，你想怎麼處理魚頭？」

「就讓培利戈切下來做魚餌吧！」

「那魚嘴呢？」

「你要的話就拿去。」

「我要，」男孩説，「現在我們要好好計畫一下別的事了。」

「他 們 有 去 找 我 嗎？」

「當然啦，海岸巡防隊和飛機都出動了。」

p. 132–133 「海洋太大了，小船又那麼小，很難找到的。」老人説。他發現現在能有個人説説話，比起在海上自言自語愉快多了。

「我很想念你。」他説，「你捕到了些什麼？」

「第一天和第二天都捕到一條，第三天兩條。」

「好極了。」

「現在我們又可以一起捕魚了。」

「不行，我運氣不好，我再也不會走運了。」

「管他什麼運氣！」男孩説，「我會帶來好運。」

「你家人會怎麼説？」

「我才不在乎呢，昨天我就捕了兩條魚，但從現在我們還是要一起捕魚，我還有好多要學，你老人家快把手給治好吧。」

「我知道要怎麼照顧我的手，昨天晚上我吐了些怪怪的東西，還覺得胸口裡好像哪裡破裂了。」

「這個也要調養好，」男孩説，「先躺下來，老先生，我會幫你拿乾淨的襯衫過來，再帶點東西給你吃。」

「給我帶一份我不在這幾天的隨便一份報紙吧。」老人説。

p. 134-135 「你一定要盡快好起來，我要學的還很多，你可以把一切都教給我。你到底受了多少罪？」

「很多！」老人説。

「我會幫你帶食物和報紙過來，」男孩説，「好好休息吧，老先生，我會去藥局幫你拿一些擦手的藥。」

小男孩走出門，到路上他又哭了起來。

那天下午，露臺酒館來了許多遊客，有個女人往水裡看，在一堆空啤酒罐和死梭魚間看到又大又長的白色脊骨，末端還矗立著巨大的尾巴，隨著潮水起漂動。

「那是什麼？」她指著大魚的長背脊骨問侍者。現在那只是一個等著被潮流沖走的垃圾。

　　「大鯊魚，」侍者說，「是鯊魚！」他想說說事情的經過。

　　「我以前都不知道鯊魚有這麼漂亮的的尾巴，樣子也這麼好看。」

　　「我也不知道。」她的男伴說道。

　　走上這條路，在他的小屋裡，老人又睡著了。他還是趴著睡，小男孩就坐在他旁邊守候著。老人又夢到獅子。

Answers

P. 50

A ❶ F ❷ F ❸ T ❹ T ❺ F ❻ F

B
❶ The old man will be hooking a huge fish.
❷ The old man will be rowing far out to sea.
❸ The tuna fish will be jumping out of the water.

P. 51

C ❷ → ❺ → ❶ → ❸ → ❹

D ❶ trousers ❷ taut ❸ current ❹ made
❺ dream

P. 94

A ❶ F ❷ T ❸ T ❹ F ❺ T

B ❶ (b) ❷ (a)

P. 95

C ❶ fillets ❷ poured ❸ as long as
❹ strange ❺ lurch

D ❹ → ❶ → ❺ → ❸ → ❷

P. 136

A ❶ T ❷ F ❸ T ❹ F ❺ T

B ❶ violated ❷ swallowed ❸ harbor
❹ pack ❺ jaws

P. 137

C ❶ (b) ❷ (d)

D ❶ -b ❷ -a ❸ -c

190

P. 142 (A) ❶ All that's left of the fish at the end of the story is a skeleton. (T)

❷ Joe DiMaggio once spoke to the old man. (F)

❸ The old man has a deep knowledge of the sea and its creatures. (T)

❹ There are many sharks waiting in the current near the shore. (T)

❺ The old man is in terrible physical shape at the end of this book. (T)

❻ The boy thinks he can't learn anything more from the old man. (F)

(B) ❶ What is this story about? (c)

❷ Why did people call the old man "The Champion" when he was young? (a)

P. 143 (C) ❶ skiff empty   ❷ through this fiction
❸ rowing steadily   ❹ convince, no match
❺ unclear   ❻ faint and sick

(D) ❶ The old man had to fish alone.

❷ The sharks ate the entire fish before the old man could get it to shore.

❸ The old man hooked into a huge marlin.

❹ The boy's parents thought the old man was unlucky.

❺ The old man finally managed to harpoon the fish.

❹ → ❶ → ❸ → ❺ → ❷

老人與海【二版】（刪節版）
The Old Man and the Sea

作者 _ 歐內斯特・海明威
　　　（Ernest Hemingway）
插圖 _ Julina Alekcangra
翻譯／編輯 _ 羅竹君／黃朝萍
作者／故事簡介翻譯 _ 王采翎
校對 _ 陳慧莉
協力編輯校對 _ 洪巧玲
封面設計 _ 林書玉
排版 _ 葳豐／林書玉
播音員 _ Michael Yancey, Mary Jones
製程管理 _ 洪巧玲
發行人 _ 周均亮
出版者 _ 寂天文化事業股份有限公司
電話 _ +886-2-2365-9739
傳真 _ +886-2-2365-9835
網址 _ www.icosmos.com.tw
讀者服務 _ onlineservice@icosmos.com.tw
出版日期 _ 2020年7月 二版一刷　　（250201）
郵撥帳號 _ 1998620-0 寂天文化事業股份有限公司

國家圖書館出版品預行編目資料

老人與海 / Ernest Hemingway 原著；羅竹君譯.
-- 二版 . -- [臺北市] : 寂天文化 , 2020.05
　　面；　　公分 . -- (Grade 5 經典文學讀本)
原著刪節版
譯自 : The old man and the sea
ISBN 978-986-318-912-1 (25K 平裝附光碟片)

1. 英語 2. 讀本

　　　805.18　　　　　　　　109005497